PRIS◉NERS

Life is a virtual prison
Choose your prison before one chooses you!

MICHELLE PAULA BARTON-ROMEO

M.P. BARTON ROMEO

PUBLICATIONS

Michelle Paula Barton-Romeo

MICHELLE PAULA BARTON-ROMEO

Unity Road, Rich Plain, Diego Martin Trinidad, W.I.

mpbromeo@yahoo.com
www.facebook.com/mpbromeo.prisoners
www.michellepaula.com

WhatsApp

1 868 360 3492

DEDICATION

This, my first book, is dedicated to everyone who has a dream.
A dream of being free to live a life that is fulfilling.
The life that you want for yourself,
realising the dreams and goals that you want to pursue,
not discounting the tests that must be passed
in order to make you, you!

I pray that you enjoy reading this book but more importantly,
that I have inspired you to break free from your prison.

ACKNOWLEDGMENTS

Firstly, and this is not a cliché, I must acknowledge and thank God for giving me the skills I needed to write and for seeing me through this entire process. I believe that good ideas are really God ideas. So thank you Father for Your leading,
thank You Holy Spirit for Your guidance
and thank You Jesus for Your grace and mercy.

I acknowledge my Pastors, Apostles Vivian and Jemma Duncan for setting the example and for "throwing me out into the deep". Your leadership has inspired me to realise my dream of becoming a writer., for this I sincerely thank you.

One day at church, I sat and listened to a message by Apostle Margaret Lee, that sermon was different, it was the basis of the inspiration for me to come up with this story. So I say thanks to Apostle Lee for giving me that inspiration as she preached a message from the heart of God.

Thanks also to Ms. Jennifer Roderique, my editor. You have encouraged me to keep on writing. Your constant uplifting words propelled me to persevere and publish.

I truly acknowledge my immediate family. Thank you for giving me the time I needed to pen my thoughts in order to produce this book. Your support is indicative of my success.

Gratitude goes out to my son, Jemuel John Romeo, for the cover design that captured my heart and the heart of this book.

Finally, I say thanks to you, the readers, for I know you will recommend this book to your friends.

May God richly bless you all!

Contents

FOREWORD

I decided to set aside some of my precious time to read the manuscript of **Prisoners**. The first time I read a few pages but, at my second attempt, I could hardly put it down and finished it in one sitting.

Here the spotlight was placed on some sacred cows of full gospel churches: things we merely whisper and gossip about; things we prefer to sweep under the carpet; things we bury and pretend will disappear. We refuse to acknowledge that these issues will not go away but that they tend to get worse as time passes.

Who in the church talks about domestic violence, infidelity, rape and incest, homosexuality among family members, promiscuity among spouses and children? We prefer to speak meaningless clichés like, "I am too blessed to be stressed", even while the ravages of stressful living are causing our very lifeblood to leak out.

Here the author dares to declare that each of us is a prisoner of one kind of problem or another; some we choose and others are inflicted upon us. Some become prisoners because of *cause and effect.*

Is this story a tragedy? Not really. Although there were some tragic episodes, we see the Mighty Hand of Almighty God moving among mortal men, helpless by themselves but empowered when they surrender to His will, ensuring that Romans 8:28 becomes a truth in their lives:

"And we know that all things work together for good to them

that love God, to them who are the called according to His purpose".

Amazingly, we will always be prisoners but the choice is ours: we can either remain in bondage or we can choose to become a prisoner of Christ.

Congratulations!

Michelle, let's raise the carpet and sweep the dust out.
Apostle Jemma, 08/07/14

Michelle Paula Barton-Romeo

4

Chapter One

A wind of change is blowing or is it that the wind has stopped blowing altogether. All is quiet on this very humid Friday evening in the middle of the year. The birds are chirping softly in the backyard. The neighbours have already returned home from work and are indoors. No one is venturing out at this time. Rufus, our pot-hound dog, is also very quiet; usually he would attempt to pounce on the insects that bother him but not today – he, too, is quite still. The water in the fountain is running as if in slow motion. I have never before noticed the formation of the water as it flows over the rocks and stones that line the concrete walls of this fabulous Egyptian masterpiece. It looks like a river flowing freely over everything and anything in its path and nothing is allowed to stop it; and so as I look, I think, 'This water represents me.'

Today I buried my husband. We had been married for almost thirty-two years. All seemed well on the outside but I wished for years that he were dead. Now that my wish had become a reality, I perceived myself to be like the water in the fountain, free spirited. I did not need to pretend anymore; I felt free to run over anything in my path that was lifeless or void of feelings. Except that now – I don't know how I feel – I don't know how I should feel. In spite of all that had happened between us, I think I'll miss him.

My sons had remained at the house with me after the funeral and planned to spend the weekend. Four young strong men who all found excuses to leave our home the minute they were able to stand on their own. I always wanted a girl, maybe she would have stayed, but I believe that God saw it fit for me to be the only female in the family. I suppose that accounts for my being so strong emotionally. Throughout my life I had adopted the mentality of men. As a matter of fact, for most of my life I lived only around men. My mother died when I was two; I have no siblings and was brought up by a single father. I have no idea if he ever dated another woman; he surely did not bring anyone home to our house; or, maybe did so only when I went to spend weekends by my Aunt. Oh how foolish and naïve I have been all my life! That's it: My father had to have gotten rid of me in order to entertain his ladies on weekends! He is not here now for me to ask him though. He too died only a couple months before I married George. After that my whole life was wrapped up in this one man and our four sons, and I just wanted him to be the only one so I stayed even though he was such a tyrant.

The funeral was quiet and peaceful. George's friends are dignified and so we just played along with them. I knew however that within me lived another being, she was like a lioness that had not eaten for days. I kept her quiet for years but now I really wanted to set her loose. The atmosphere at the house was solemn. I think we still could not believe that George was really gone. I had planned to pretend for a little while longer before I showed the world how happy I was.

The last time we had all been together in this house, the home we shared when they were kids, were many, many years prior to George's death. Everyone, except for André, is grown and gone. For the most part, we only talk to each other on the phone.

André, the third of my sons, moved back home about two years before his father died, when he heard how sick he was. He had ended a relationship with someone I thought was the best thing that had ever happened to him and he lived alone in San Fernando. Aphelia, the daughter of my best friend, Sonja, is an exquisitely beautiful, yet simple young woman. She wears clothing that fit her perfectly, never too tight or too short. The latest styles do not burn her eyes and she never shows her mid-section or any cleavage. She enjoys a little drink now and again but does not allow herself to get drunk. Her curly, bronze-coloured hair is always pinned up in a smooth round bun, and coming to think of it I have no idea what the real length is because I have never seen her with her hair let down. André and Aphelia lived together in San Fernando although they both grew up right here in Woodbrook. They worked together in Administration at one of the Petroleum companies in the south.

André says that he 'found Jesus'. I didn't know that He was lost, but that is the reason why he broke up with Aphelia. She resigned her job shortly afterwards and went to New York to meet her mother; but he is still employed there driving to and from San Fernando every day to go to work. I stopped asking André questions about his relationship because he would give me the same stupid answers. However, I have never seen anyone sadder. Well, only as far as having a girlfriend is concerned; otherwise, I think he is the most stable child that I have.

There must be something about this Christian thing. He has truly changed over the years and I see a level of happiness in him that seems to be unconditional. No girlfriend, a father who hated him and wanted him to move back out; yet he was able to smile, not the pretend smile that I know I portray most of the time, but a genuine smile that says: 'I am satisfied with my life'. I really cannot comprehend how he does it but he does.

Anthony, my eldest, is an executive, the business man of the family. After completing A-level examinations at Fatima College, Anthony went directly to the University of the West Indies, Mona campus in Jamaica, where he studied Geology. He now has two Masters Degrees and is working on his Doctorate. Anthony is thirty-one years old; George and I got pregnant with him two months before our wedding. After my over protective father died I simply could not wait to have sex. I was only eighteen. We did it without thinking and I got pregnant immediately. Hence the reason we married so soon after daddy's death and, well I inherited the house, so George just moved right in.

Anthony had worked really hard to acquire a scholarship to go to Jamaica. He could not live with his father anymore. When he returned to Trinidad, he was put up in a company house and never came back home. He is now a Manager in one of the Government's leading subsidiaries in the oil sector. He was influential in assisting André and Aphelia with getting jobs.

Anton is my second son. He is really very bright and extremely handsome. All the girls chase after him and he just loves it. I don't think he ever had a steady girlfriend and I can't imagine where all these girls come from. George and I never allowed the boys to bring girls home to overnight so Anton got an apartment and moved out since he was about twenty years old. His computer skills allowed him to land a pretty good job as an Information Technology Specialist, and he teaches additional classes on afternoons. Anton needs a lot of money to support his ridiculously expensive lifestyle. All he does with his money is pay rent, dress to kill, drive a red sports car and party his life away on the weekends.

My youngest, Anderson, is definitely the child that I am most ashamed of. Academically, he turned out really well and is a Junior Accountant with an international accountancy firm. He is effeminate though and it kills me. I sometimes have nightmares when I recall a conversation that sent my blood pressure through the roof. I was getting ready to attend his wedding, for although Anderson was the youngest, he had the first, actually the only wedding thus far in this family. I was so excited about this wedding and being the mother of the groom, I chose a dress that was divine: gold and pearl in colour, cut just under the breast and flowing to floor length in a semi-flare skirt; sequins lined the upper bodice and the thin straps were made of infinitesimal gold roses; an iridescent georgette shawl draped across my shoulders. The jewelry also was a rare exquisite design that only someone with the status of Cleopatra would wear. It was a genuine pearl necklace with matching earrings; between each pearl there were beads of gold and rubies. Good God, I felt like a million dollars.

Then the telephone rang. Anderson was on the other end, crying and sobbing with such deep grunts, like a sow in labour. He was inconsolable. I thought that Marlene had cancelled the wedding. To my surprise however, the wedding had been cancelled yes, but it was Anderson who had cancelled it. He then disclosed to me that he was different, gay, homosexual, funny. However you said it, it all sounded reprehensible. Anderson said he had tried to be normal but he simply couldn't, so he decided to call the wedding off. I was speechless at first; I could not believe my ears; but then I screamed and cursed in a manner I myself did not know I was capable of. The audacity of this boy to embarrass this family with such ludicrousness! (As if people were to know my truth, I would be blameless). We saw him three days later when he came to the house to collect some stuff.

Marlene was a wreck, but picked up the pieces of her life and moved on. She has since married and has two children. Although we all know that Anderson likes his own 'kind', we rarely talk about it. I know for certain that he is unhappy though; just a mother's instinct since he hasn't revealed anything to me.

After having four children in four years, I tied my tubes. That was it for me, but I do love my boys with all my heart. Though our conversations took place over the phone most times, we had a very good relationship. I think I did a great job — each one of them is well qualified. Thankfully, finances have never been a problem for this family so we had everything we needed to take care of our physical needs. We were starved emotionally though; something that money cannot buy. I was now going to live on all that I was entitled to, being George's wife: his pension, his savings, the mutual funds, and the Government Bonds. What a life! I have everything I want, so why am I not happy, I wonder?

It is so amazing how much the human mind can expand to accommodate our wildest thoughts. I guess we do live our lives in our minds first. As I looked around I saw my sons sitting there so quietly but I knew that their minds are racing as fast as mine was. I know that they were each hoping that they could rewrite history. At least they could enjoy pleasant thoughts, even if it was just for a while.

Chapter Two

y life was filled with drama. Funny enough, I did not grow up with problems like these; I had a pretty good childhood. I mean, daddy watched me like a hawk but that's what good fathers do for their little girls. I cannot remember my mother too much at all; I was way too young when she passed. When I look at the pictures, I know that somehow I know this lady but I cannot tell in what way. When I was sixteen, my father finally told me how she died. He said that one day she complained of excruciating pain in her abdomen and was taken to the hospital. The doctors took her away quickly and when they returned they said that they tried everything they could but were unable to save her. She had had an ectopic pregnancy and her left fallopian tube exploded as the fetus grew too large for it. Daddy said he did not even know she was pregnant again and he believes that she didn't know either. However, he never got the chance to ask her. I could not help but think that I missed out on a little brother or sister and my mother. I felt cheated in some way but thought that God probably had a good reason.

I met George at our school's Christmas fundraiser when I was in form five. He had just started working with the insurance firm that sponsored a number of our projects. St. Francois Girls' High School was noted for their fabulous events and this yearly event was their biggest. I have some rather sweet memories of that day and there are times that I returned to it so that I could remember him in the way I saw him at first. During the after-party, as we all stood lingering around in our pretty dresses, Sonja brought me a drink, my absolute favorite drink, a strawberry splash with fruit cocktail. She even added the umbrella and a long stemmed cherry and I could smell a hint of aged rum emanating from the mix. She knew I just loved it but Daddy thought that I was drinking a simple fruit punch. She handed me the drink, jerked her head in the direction of the salad bar and said, "Compliments of the cute guy who cannot take his eyes off you." I looked towards the salad bar and saw a stunningly handsome young man smiling at me. I smiled back shyly, batted my eyes and turned away. He knew that all that meant was, 'Come on over. I'll talk to you.' We 'hit it off' immediately; falling in love at first sight. That disease is usually cured with a second look but I guess I forgot to look twice.

George was really very sweet. He would meet me almost everyday after school and walk me into Port of Spain to get a taxi to go home. I valued those times and soon he became my best friend; we discussed everything and anything. Sonja was a little jealous because he took away some of our time. She did understand though because she knew that I could not take him home to Daddy; at least not yet. George and I did include her some days and he treated us both to snow cones or ice cream. This was our routine for a little over a year, and then Daddy died.

I should have known that something was terribly wrong with George because he never talked about family. All he told me was that he was an orphan, born to unmarried drug addicts and was given up at birth to live in an orphanage. His mother had died in childbirth and he never knew the identity of his father. George left the orphanage at eighteen and made a life for himself afterwards – a very good life as far as a career was concerned. He was well-respected on the job and moved up the ranks all the way to C.E.O. Who would have thought that he would turn out to be the man that I hated most in this world? He was supposed to be my darling husband but our relationship went sour within a few years.

When we got married, I decided to stay at home with the kids and be a home-maker; not that I could not get a job. I did perform well at school and had graduated with seven O'level subjects, it was just a choice I made; I wanted to take care of my kids for myself. My hopes for a degree were dashed as Daddy fell ill in my first year of Advanced Level studies and I gave up furthering my education so I could stay at home to care for him.

I remember it all. He was deteriorating rapidly. The doctors said that there was no hope. Daddy had been a chain smoker. Eventually, he suffered from lung cancer and emphysema. By the time he had gotten himself checked out, the cancer had already spread to other important organs and it was too late. He was strong enough to put all his financial issues in order so that when he departed this life I could go on with mine. He was concerned because I was pretty much all that was left of our family. My mom was an only child. Daddy had one sister who lived in a home for the aged. She didn't know me anymore. Alzheimer's took all our memories away. She eventually died a few months after my father.

Daddy had left me a pretty good amount of money and the house. He also advised me to hide most of the money in a place that no one could find it. He said that if I had no family I should be extra careful as I was on my own. And so I placed most of the money in a private account. I did not tell George anything about the account so he thought that the amount I showed him was all I had. George only knew what I wanted him to know. He had an excellent paying job, though, so there was really no need to even discuss that money.

Our major troubles began when I caught him in our bed with another woman. That was the fatal mistake, the final straw, and since that day I could not be intimate with him again. During the first few years of marriage it seemed like I was pregnant all the time. George had become impatient with me as I really was not in the mood for much intimacy and so he began to look elsewhere to satisfy his sexual needs. I thought he would have stopped the tyranny because after the last child went off to pre-school I was a lot better. I returned to my old sexy self again, but by that time he was hooked. Six years into the marriage and he was still sleeping with many women; really they were little girls, because it seemed that each time he found a new girlfriend she was even younger than the previous one. I knew he was being unfaithful, I knew that many of the nights he said he was out of town on company business was really spent in various hotel rooms while I cried myself to sleep. I prayed and hoped that things would get better between us. Well, things did not get any better. I flipped that day because I could not stand the thought of him in my bed with someone else; and so I never allowed him to touch me again.

It was Christmas time and I was out shopping with the boys. I told George that I would carry them to San Fernando to shop that day. San Fernando's most prestigious mall, Gulf City, had a fantastic play area and I thought they would have lots of fun; we were planning to be out all day. I had stopped by Sonja's house before heading to San Fernando when I accidentally locked the keys in the car. She offered to watch the boys for me and I taxied home to get the spare set of keys.

When I reached home I was surprised to see George's car. George . . . at home? I found that to be strange because he said he could not get the day off to go with us. There was a blue car parked outside our house as well, but other people park there all the time so I did not think too much of it. We usually kept another set of house keys hidden just in case we lost our copies so I used those to get in the house. Upon entering my home, I heard a little chuckle, at first I thought it was the television but then I heard George's voice and someone else's in giggly conversation. I did assume the worst but hoped that I was mistaken. I slowly walked in the direction of the voices which led to our bedroom. The tears welled up, my heart began to beat so fast and so powerfully I thought it would burst through my chest. I turned around. I thought it might just be best to break open my car, forget about the spare keys. But then, I thought, am I not Mrs. Graham? I am the only woman that is supposed to be in that bedroom. HELL NO! Not in my house. Not in my bed. Walking as fast as I could, each step angrier than the last, I flung the door open; it hit the wall with a crash, various layers of wall paint sprinkled to the floor leaving a circle of bare concrete on the wall. Both parties jumped up and spun around, their faces showing astounding expressions of horror.

Oh, the shock on that poor child's face; she couldn't be more than nineteen. She was up first and without saying anything, pulled up her underwear and got dressed faster than Superman ever could. She walked up to me with her shoes in her hand and she opened her mouth to say something, but only God knew what that was, because before she could say a word, I smashed her mouth with my fist. I have a bad right hand and wore my school ring on my fore-finger. The ring knocked out a tooth and she screamed in pain. George got up and started to yell at me: "What the hell are you doing?" he said. "Come after me, not her!" I stood still and silent and she just walked out of the house, into her car and drove off.

Ooh ... I was just waiting for him to go after her and not stay there and talk to me. I'm certain the rage that came over me at that moment would have turned me into a murderer. George knew that I was beyond angry and he calmed himself immediately and tried to talk but I would not let him. Everything he said bounced off; I answered not a word. "Melinda, I am so sorry ... I do love you ... I, I ..."

Still I answered not a word. I walked away, stomping to my drawer to get the spare key for my car. George, still half naked, came behind and placed his hands on my shoulders. His touch was so tender, I breathed in deeply and for a very brief moment I thought I should just show him that I can deliver something that no other woman could. I felt that at this point I had the power to get my husband to crave for me and only me. In that moment I also saw flashes of our erotically explosive sexual encounters, but not even that could sooth my temper.

I roughly shrugged his hands off my shoulders and yelled: "Don't touch me!" I stormed out of the bedroom and headed straight for the front door. He came at me again: "Please, Melinda, let's talk about this ... I am sorry ... I want to stop. I promise to stop. Give me another chance; if not for me, for our boys."

That last statement hit me like a ton of bricks: "For our boys!" I screamed, "You did not think about our boys, George. I begged you to take the day off to spend time with me and the boys and like a million times before you lied. Having sex with someone's baby sister in my bed was more important to you than us. Don't you dare tell me anything about our boys!"

George begged - it was the first time I had seen him so desperate. He knew he had pushed me over the edge this time. "Melinda, I'm sorry, I don't know what I was thinking ... I will get help..."

At this point I was so fed up with all this nonsense, I just told him off. As I opened the door to leave I warned him angrily: "If I ever catch you in my house with anyone again, I will kill you." He became enraged and I saw a side of George that I had never seen before. He grabbed me with one hand and pulled me inside the house, slamming the front door. The glass cracked. I was scared but I was too angry to show it. With his other hand he held my chin and forcefully tilting it upwards he spoke in my face, his breath registering each word as he spoke:

"Just remember woman, this house was a little two-bedroom shack and I made it into a palace. I own this house as much as you do and I will not leave, so don't ever refer to it as your house again. I won't tell you what I'll do but I know you won't like it."

With that threat he released me and walked away. George had never threatened me before. My anger must have triggered it but I did not care. I was very afraid but just left and went to get the kids.

I have no clue how I was able to pull myself together, collect the boys and not even Sonja could tell that something was wrong. It was two months before I told her anything. I did not go home that night; I did not go to San Fernando either. Instead I went straight to

17

the bank, to my private account; drew out some money, drove to the airport, got on a plane, destination: Tobago. This was a huge step for me, I had never been to Tobago and I have never been on an airplane.

The boys were a little confused. I told them that Daddy got called away from Trinidad on a business trip and I thought it would be best to spend Christmas away from home. In Tobago I rented a car and a self-contained bungalow close to the beach. I made friends with one of the staff members and she took us shopping; we needed everything. Hermin was really sweet and I had to talk to somebody so I told her a lot of what I was going through. She was like a personal assistant to me and for that I was very grateful. The boys spent the rest of the day in the water so they were really contented with the impromptu decision to spend Christmas in Tobago - clean, green, safe, and serene Tobago - with its fabulous beaches and long stretches of sand. The island is much smaller than Trinidad with fewer people and much less traffic; a very peaceful place to be.

I put the boys to bed but stayed up half the night. The waves crashing on the shore provided background music for my 'drama presentation' - my true life drama presentation. I starred in the show but had no clue what to portray next. I cried so much that my heart ached. Why? Why? Why did George have to be like this? How could I not see that he was a player? The pain was unbearable but the atmosphere of the sister isle was soothing to my weary soul. When I could not cry anymore I decided to be at peace - sheer peace.

This peace was short lived. I called George early the next morning and told him not to look for me. I called to prevent him from reporting his family missing. I did say that I was in Tobago. He asked what I had said to the boys and I told him. To my surprise he actually found us in Tobago that very day. He came, too, because he knew that I would never behave badly in front of the kids and, of course, I pretended that all was well. He told the boys he had cancelled his trip because he felt bad not to be with his family for Christmas and lah-de-dah-de-dah. He spent the night with us and practically ordered me to return home with him. We left the following day. I never saw Hermin again. I did not even have a number for her. I missed her but was more concerned about whether or not she would tell my story. I prayed that she would keep it to herself.

Back at home that night, George put the boys to bed. I watched his every move; ever so often he glanced in my direction, hoping that his stares would break me, longing for the opportunity to talk to me. I was still intensely angry, deeply hurt and profoundly upset; giving in to George was not on my agenda. There is a thin line between love and hate and he had crossed that line. I felt hatred for him now.

George took vacation for the Christmas holidays and never left our sight. The boys were very happy; I hid all that was happening from them. I should be in Hollywood – I am such a great actress! None of our friends had a clue that we were in this mess. George tried to talk to me every chance he got. He tried hard to fix the problem but I was unrelenting and did not concede at all. I thought he should be punished for a long, long time. I still refused to let him touch me. Christmas passed, the New Year rang in, Carnival, Easter, I kept firm in my stance – I was not going to sleep with him. Sex is sacred to me. I tolerated his infidelity and hoped that it would end, but why did he defile our home? That action was unforgivable.

My rigid decision, however, gave way to his being incredibly vicious and malevolent towards me. I could not have imagined that George was anything like that. It was an almost unbearable experience, one I would not wish on my worst enemy. I had kept sex off my agenda for more than a year. Then one day we attended another function, his office's annual Carnival party. There I would usually meet his co-workers. One of them made a bad joke, although he had no clue that it was. He told George that I was looking like I was still eighteen and he bet that sex was even better now than then. I think the fact that another man found me appealing and that I had kept myself from him triggered something.

That night George begged me to be with him again; I still refused. I did feel sorry but could not get the image of his infidelity out of my mind; and to make matters worse, although he tried desperately to make things better between us, he still slept around. However, after apologising and apologising for months to no avail, he had had enough and decided to show me 'who is boss'. He could no longer handle my constant rejection; his temper had reached boiling point. Then the unthinkable happened - he raped me repeatedly that night. I endured what seemed like hours of torture. I felt a barrage of feelings all at once – degradation, humiliation, mortification, and chagrin. It happened just as we began to argue. We did not agree on anything anymore, I had lost my friend, I had lost George. I did not know who this man was. His voice got louder and louder:

"Keep your voice down!" I demanded. "You will wake the kids."

"I don't care anymore. How long will you punish me?" he asked harshly.

"For as long as I want to. You have not changed."

"I have given you everything you ever wanted."

"Sure, everything I wanted but the one thing I needed you withheld. Monogamy, faithfulness, Jesus, George, you still sleep with countless women!"

"Well, I am not getting sex from you."

"Don't you dare put this on me. You have been sleeping around since our first year of marriage."

"You got pregnant before we were married and then you lost interest in sex."

"Did I get pregnant on my own? Or did you not passionately make love to me? We were kids; we made a mistake not using protection. You talk like I got pregnant on purpose."

"Well, did you? Your father died and left you all alone. You forced me to marry you. I was not ready."

"Oh, just shut up, fool. I hate the very ground you walk on!" I went to bed, pulled the covers over me and I left him standing there. Suddenly I felt the covers ripped off me and before I even realised what was going on, he jumped on top of me.

"You are still my wife! You cannot say no!"

"Yes I can. Get off me! Get off me!"

I struggled a bit but he was too strong and so he overpowered me and raped me. I begged him to leave me alone; he held me down even tighter. The pain was horrible, both physically and emotionally. I hated him even more, but I did not know how to handle the situation. I wanted my father – he had always protected me – but he was dead. I wanted to die but that thought vanished when my sons' names flashed across my mind: Anthony, Anton, André, and Anderson. Melinda you must live for them. Be strong. You must live for the boys. I crawled up into a corner of the room and cried until my head hurt. George was heartless: he sat on the bed and watched me cry. He teased me and said things to hurt me even more.

"I will take whatever I want, and whenever I want it from you. I will sleep with whomever I want to. Who the hell you think you are to tell me what to do? How powerful do you feel now?"

I did not go back into the bed. I stayed on the floor and cried all night. George did not sleep either – maybe he was too afraid of being vulnerable. He talked all the time – hurling insults – things that a woman should never hear a man say at all; but I did not answer. Two hours later, he raped me again. The hatred in my heart grew stronger. I thought only of my kids and I made up my mind, even in the pain, to be strong and courageous. I was helpless but not hopeless. I had no family and very few friends. Who would I turn to? This is the only home I knew; where would I go? I purposely thought about all of this and tried to come up with a solution.

Something happened to George that night. Satan must have released a couple hundred demons on him; I thought, 'This is not my George'. This man has got to be possessed by something. This was a really bad guy like the ones we see in the movies - an animal in the depths of the forest; definitely something else! This could not be my husband. I survived the night and the following days, though crying, contemplating, wondering what to make of all this mess. I was devastated but decided to just live.

The rapes did not stop there but continued at least

twice a week or so thereafter. People think that there must be violence in order to confirm rape. However violence occurs mostly when the victim fights back. Except for the first few times, George was never physically violent per se. He was indignant! He just demanded that I get undressed and then demanded that he be allowed to penetrate. He planned this. He always had a good supply of KY Jelly at all times. He had to, without a doubt I was never turned on. I had forgotten what that felt like. His view was that wives just cannot say no and as far as he was concerned, he owned my body. That was rape! My clothing was never ripped nor was I slapped or beaten and he did not hold a knife to my neck. It did not matter though. I was raped!

I decided not to ever fight it, but just left him to do whatever he wanted. I thought if I did fight he would hit me one day and that would leave bruises. The boys would then find out and I was determined that they were never to find out. My face would be drenched in tears each time, but I never cried aloud. The hurt was severe. I felt like I would die; but my sons, I had to live for my sons. Before I could figure out how to handle the situation, I got accustomed to it. I still cannot fathom how he was able to do it though, nor can I comprehend how I was able to function, but I did. Maybe I should have thrown him out of the house; I couldn't do that either. He did tell me it was as much his as mine. I could have left, but I have no clue why I stayed – a prisoner in my own home! I guess I was just keeping up appearances. I did have a life outside of that marriage. So I bore it but secretly, I wished he were dead.

Whenever I had to accompany George on one of his "show-off-your-spouse" dinners or luncheons, we would be so lovey-dovey that people really did not think that there was a problem. Every other aspect of our relationship functioned quite normally. We kept the bedroom prison a secret. One can hide from everyone on the outside the problems that exist on the inside, but I could not hide from myself. In my quiet times when no one saw me, when no one could hear me, I was a wreck. I fed my pain in tears and anguish. I tried to call on God but I did not know how. I felt alone in my pain and so I wanted George dead.

I tried my best to keep my family together in spite of the deviltries that I had faced. However, it was not long before George began to resent the boys as well. That resentment was a direct result of his guilt because I made certain not to reveal anything to them at all. I believed that up until his death they still had no clue as to what I had gone through. They each had their own challenges with their father and thought that he simply did not like them.

Anthony took the situation with his father the hardest. He was irretrievably hurt by George when he was seventeen and never bounced back totally. He was above average at school and placed first in end-of-term examinations on every occasion but one. That one time he didn't, was the time he fell ill and was vomiting profusely. He had two more exams to complete and still made it to school but had to return home without even seeing the exam paper. George really could not find much fault in Anthony and so he thought he finally had an opportunity to hurt him. After viewing the report he told Anthony that he was so disgusted with it he would cut him off from his inheritance. I have never seen a child express shock like Anthony did that day. I could have picked up his face off the floor.

He was preparing for C.X.C. examinations at the time. I had to motivate him continuously just so he could make it through. He was so depressed that one day I tried to cheer him up by showing him a statement

24

with the money that my father left me. It had doubled by that time and I was extremely excited about it. Anthony looked at me sorrowfully, knowing full well that I would not like what he was about to say: "Mom, I know that I am very brilliant, I can make my own money. I just can't believe that my own father would treat me like this." He felt this was the worst thing he had ever experienced. It was that evening he informed me that he would work even harder to secure a scholarship then go far away to study; and so he completed the C.X.C. exams, acquired six distinctions and three credits. At Advanced Level he again performed with excellence, got the scholarship then left home. Not long afterwards the other children all found reasons to leave home as well.

I loathed the empty nest. I would do anything that I could to be with my boys. At least when they were here I had something else to focus on besides the horrendous rapes which continued until about a year before George fell ill; although the abuse lessened somewhat over the years. I believe that George thought I had accepted the situation because I never argued, fought or even talked to him about my feelings. I did absolutely nothing to annoy him. I was such a good wife: I washed, cooked, took care of the house and did everything else a wife would do, except have sex willingly.

George always looked his best as well. It's funny that I saw to it that he looked good all the time and ironically it was never for me, but for all the whores in town. I still cannot understand how he could be so blind. How could he not have known that this was evil? How could he not care that he destroyed my dreams of a happy marriage, a normal life? And how could he not know that I loved him?

I had so many unanswered questions, so much pain,

that I wondered if there was a God at all. There were times when I felt there really had been a "big bang" because I thought that there could not be a supreme being who just stood by and watched me go through all of this alone. At other times I thought that this was just my fate. All the same, although the rapes lessened to almost naught by this time, I still practically demanded of God to let George die. For me there was no forgiveness for what he had done.

The night that George told me he was sick was one of the best nights of my life. On hearing the news, I was cold and harsh and it was the first time that I revealed to George how hurt I was. He came home that day with his face touching the ground. I knew something was terribly wrong but as long as I smelled perfume that did not belong to me I would administer an anesthetic to my heart and pretend that nothing hurt. I went to bed about an hour before he did that night but was not asleep when he came in. He sat at the edge of our luxurious queen-sized divan that had been turned into a bed of oppression. I knew he had something to say but waited for him to bring it up.

"Melinda," he called softly to see if I was awake.

"Yeah," I replied, then turned towards him.

"I have prostate cancer. I knew since last year. The treatments worked for a while but today the doctor said that I must have surgery."

I became numb – no wonder the rapes had ceased. He was being treated for cancer and had lost his sexual appetite. His announcement did not soften me. I felt only contempt for him when he shared his news. My entire life flashed before my eyes in a split second and I thought that finally I had the chance to tell George how I really felt. Incredibly, I loved him; even with his evil ways I loved him, but I wanted to hurt him as much as he hurt me and I used this opportunity to do so. For the first time in over twenty years I felt like I had the upper hand and although I felt badly for him, I was going to make him suffer some more: "Well," I said taking my time to dig into his heart with some seriously harsh words, "it is about time something curbed your sexual appetite. Now you cannot hurt me anymore. Maybe now you will leave me in peace, don't you think?"

I knew I had him; he looked at me and could not say a word. It had been so many years of pain and I never told him how hurt I was but I believe he knew that he had taken away something from me. He did take a lot but I remained strong through it all and lived a great life. George was far away in thought and stared into my eyes. The gawk etched on his face begged for mercy but he was too proud to ask for it with his heart, or his lips. I broke into his concentration with even more piercing words. "What the hell you looking at me like that for? Have you counted how many times you raped me? Do you know how much money I spent on preventative medication just in case you contracted whatever, from your whores and gave it to me? I have had to combat yeast infections almost every month. I take an AIDS test every six months because I simply don't know what you have. Do you even care that you chased my children from this home and I barely see them? I have waited for you to die so that I can be free. So even if you live, at least your penis should die! They should just cut your balls off! There is a God in heaven after all!"

I tried to be brave but honestly wondered if I had angered him and if he would retaliate. He did nothing, he said nothing. He just stood up, removed his robe and went to bed. I could only imagine what was going through his mind. Maybe if he apologised this time I would simmer down but George's heart was already

27

cemented in stone. It was good that I did not hold my breath waiting for an apology from him because he never gave one. As he pulled the covers over his body, I had one final thing to say to him: "I hate you George, but I will take care of you. I'm not going anywhere." He still did not utter a single word from his lips and it was not long before he began to snore.

I remained awake for a while wondering what all of this really meant. I had no clue what was in store for us at that time. I finally fell asleep a couple of hours afterwards. It seemed like only five minutes though, because soon my alarm woke me up. Every morning I would be up before dawn, sit in my rocker sipping a cup of coffee at my window; I would then watch the sun rise in the eastern sky. It was the only thing that reminded me of God and I did it to keep my sanity intact.

Today was a little different; George was up before me and was already in the shower. I couldn't wait to see his face. I wondered how he slept last night, knowing that he may very well lose the part of his body that defined his character. Served him right, I thought; the monster! He came back into the bedroom and without even saying good morning he casually said:

"Today is the surgery, are you coming with me to the hospital?"

I thought to myself, 'This man is a log. He just cannot be human.'

"What time is the surgery?"

"9:00 a.m., but I have to get there at six."

"What hospital are you going to?"

"Are you coming or not? Does it really matter the time

or the place? Just get ready now."

Well, I was still the good wife and so I did get up and got dressed and we were out of the house in about an hour. George was very quiet as he drove. He was deep in thought and scared, but refused to let me know the extent of his fear. I really thought that I was just accompanying George to the hospital for a simple surgery and it would all be over. Little did I know that George would never work again, he would never walk again and he would never leave the house again.

We got to the hospital and everything was in place but something else was wrong, very wrong, and the doctors did not know until they actually put the scalpel to his skin for the surgery. They had planned to do a simple Orchidectomy but when they opened him up they realised that the cancer had spread far; it was already in the bone and had begun to affect the spinal cord. George had developed Spinal Leptomeningeal Metastases. The Orchidectomy would not help in this case and they needed to do more but there were risks involved. They now had to get my permission so they came to the waiting room, explained the risks and also indicated that although they had done this surgery many times, there was only one patient who was unable to walk afterwards. I gave written consent and told them to do whatever they needed to.

I waited for about seven hours but it seemed like a lifetime. I must have read every magazine on the coffee table in the waiting room. I scrutinized every picture that hung on the tall walls, and in my head, repainted all the areas on the walls that had been dirtied by people touching as they passed by. I was beginning to run out of things to do when the doctors came back into the waiting room. I did not like the look on their faces at all; they looked worried. Dr. Maharaj, who was the main doctor who had led the team of surgeons started by saying he had no clue how George had not been complaining of severe pain. Maybe he had been in pain but remember I was like a tool to him – a piece of equipment. He used me but never consulted me before use, much less about anything serious. He did his own thing and I did mine. I did not want them to know that though so I replied: "George never wanted to burden me too much, so I guess he bore it secretly." I was really getting tired of covering up for him but by now I was so far gone that I had to continue the charade. Dr. Maharaj made a different face and I knew terrible news was coming. Before he mustered courage to say anything, I asked about the outcome of the surgery:

"Did he make it through the surgery?"

"Yes, Mrs. Graham, he did but that's not the issue."

He sighed deeply before continuing, "We had to remove three massive growths that were pressing against the spinal cord. We will not know if there is any damage to his spinal cord that can cause paralysis until he wakes up. Remember also that he was unaware as to how much the cancer had spread and so we have a lot of explaining to do as well."

"When do you suppose he'll get up?"

"He will be awake soon but won't be able to converse coherently. So we better wait until tomorrow to talk to him about his condition."

"Okay," I muttered.

I had about a million questions on my mind. I was so mean to him the night before and wished I could take back all that I had said but it was too late. Dr. Maharaj was not finished talking to me yet and he wanted to get the rest of the conversation over with.

"There's one more thing, Mrs. Graham."

"Yes," I replied, thinking that he was about to tell me about some routine treatment or something.

"At this stage of the cancer we do not expect him to live much longer. He has approximately nine months to a year left. I'm sorry."

"That's it!" I cried, feeling even worse than before because of how I had treated him.

"Any further surgeries won't make much difference and will only aggravate his condition. It is best that you enjoy the rest of the time together rather than put him through sheer hell that won't lengthen the time."

"Oh, my God!" I shrieked as my eyes filled with tears.

I was falling apart. I wished him dead but had no idea that it would really happen. Dr. Maharaj spoke as if he was certain we had a wonderful relationship: "Enjoy the rest of the time together."

"Oh please, what's there to enjoy?" I thought. My tears had given him the wrong impression.

"Can I see him now?"

"Mrs. Graham, you should really get some rest. Come back tomorrow."

There was nothing and no one to go home to so I decided to stay at the hospital.

"It's okay, doctor. I'll just wait till he comes to."

"Well, if you really want to do that, it's fine. There is a very comfortable chair that reclines in the room. Come with me, I'll get a nurse to take care of you. But please, do not discuss anything without us, okay"

"Okay."

I really did not know what to think at that moment, and then I remembered that this man had four sons. I wanted to call them but was unsure of what I should do. The relationship between George and his sons was virtually non-existent. They would call him but he would refuse to talk to them. I decided to wait until George was awake before I did anything else. I tried to ditch a feeling that was welling up inside me – the one that wanted George dead so badly. Why was I being reminded of my previous thoughts? I felt that maybe I should repent but how on earth do I do that?

The nurse got me linens and helped me to settle. I was really very tired and tried my best to fall asleep so that I could get some much needed rest. My mind had been working non-stop for years and at this point I just wanted some rest, some peace. I was exhausted.

George's groans woke me around 4:00 a.m. I had to call the doctors because he was in excruciating pain. They gave him a very strong dose of morphine and he went back to sleep almost immediately. I, on the other hand, could not go back to sleep at all. My head was full and I wondered what would happen when George found out that he was dying.

Hours later, the doctors came in for their regular morning visit. George was still asleep so they decided not to wake him and allowed him to sleep a little longer. I sat there and watched him as our life replayed slowly in my head. Finally he woke up around 10:00 o'clock that morning. All he asked for at first was breakfast. The nurses brought him something to eat, raised the head of his bed so that he reached his tray comfortably and told him that he should not try to get up. His doctors were also called immediately. This is the moment for which they waited, to see if there was any sign of damage to his spine and consequent paralysis.

Dr. Maharaj arrived when George was still having breakfast and chatted with him a little. He then began to examine him. I noticed his every move. Without telling George anything, he pressed against his legs and hoped for a reaction – there was none. He began to tell George their findings. George was turning red. He allowed Dr. Maharaj to check for paralysis and realised that there was no feeling at all in his legs. The Doctor further examined him to see how far up was affected and found out that George was paralyzed from the waist down. I know George and though he tried to keep it together in front of the doctors I was expecting him to rant and rave at me in their absence.

Dr. Maharaj said they had to keep him a lot longer than planned, to run various tests. When he left, George put a cursing on me that I will never forget. He accused me of signing away his life and blamed me for his condition. He said that there had to be another way but the moment he was vulnerable I took advantage of him. Imagine that! I let him talk and talk and talk some more and when he was finished I picked up my stuff and walked out. I did not say anything and I did not go back to the hospital for eight days.

During that time I arranged a conference call with my sons to discuss the situation. There was silence on the phone as they could hardly believe their ears. We planned to meet at the hospital the next time I visited George.

When I finally went back to check on him, he was just as nasty. Our relationship was no secret to Dr.

Maharaj anymore. I asked questions but he did not answer. He did not know that Dr. Maharaj called me daily and I knew everything. So his not answering my questions was really pointless. I then revealed to him that his sons were outside. It was no surprise when George simply said, "Tell them to go home. I don't need them."

"Why in God's name are you so incredibly nasty? Do you have human blood running through your veins?" I bellowed.

"I couldn't care less what you say."

"I know! In any event I will not tell them to go home - you can tell them yourself."

When the boys got there George still insisted that he did not want to see them. I let them in anyway and they tried to talk to their father but he only answered yes, no, or shrugged his shoulders. They could not get through at all; it was useless.

They left about half an hour later and I gave George a good piece of my mind: "All I ever wanted from you was friendship, companionship and love. All I got was infidelity, abuse, neglect, and did I say abuse? It has been a nightmare living with you and God knows, had it not been for the children, I would have left you a long time ago."

"Melinda, I don't care. My life is over now."

"What life? You call that a life? What happened to you, George? Where are your whores now? We were great together. I am the mother of your kids. I am your wife, for God's sake. I love you. But you cannot love, can you?"

He obviously thought about what I had said but

would not give in – not in the least.

"What is love, Melinda? There is no such thing."

"So were you pretending to know what love is?"

"I did what I needed to do to get you to fall for me. I never wanted kids. You made four of them. They took you from me and then you took yourself from me. But you blame me for everything."

"I loved you! You reciprocated; at least, I thought you did! Those young men are the result of love. Have you ever seen me with another man? Have I not been completely devoted to you? You are a wicked soul. I wish you rot in Hell. How dare you even suggest such a thing? All you needed to do was to be patient until the child-bearing years were over. You never told me you did not want kids!" George closed his eyes and I realised that everything I was saying was just pointless now. I stopped; it was no use. After complete silence for about fifteen minutes he began to talk again.

"The doctors say that I can go home in a few days."

"So," I replied, "can you care for yourself?"

"You know that I can't."

"So is there anything you would like to ask of me?"

"Just take me home and let me die. I already refused radiation. I want to die! Get me the cheque book; I will sign all the cheques in it. Take the credit cards and the Linx cards. Take it all and don't bother me anymore. Just let me die!"

"Talk about a heart of stone." I answered candidly.

"I hope you did not tell anyone about my situation."

"I know you too well, stupid. I will not tell anyone. But let's get something straight. You will respect me starting from now. I will not tolerate this crap from you anymore."

"Fine, whatever!" That was his answer. The bitterness in George's heart gave the bitterest soul hard competition.

That was the beginning of the end of George. From that day, I cared for him till the day he died. He was as mean a being on his death bed as he was that day in the hospital. He never spoke to his kids and when André moved back in with us, he practically cursed him every day. The doctors gave him nine months but he lasted two years. I took care of him myself - I did not hire a nurse or maid. If I needed to leave the house I did so when André was at home.

He did sign all the cheques in the cheque book and gave me all the numbers to his various debit cards. I paid off all his bills and the credit cards then transferred the rest of the money to my personal account. At least he did not keep any material thing from me but freely gave up everything, even signing over the government bonds, fixed deposits and the accounts from the mutual funds. As before, money was never a problem where George was concerned; I always had money. He always gave me money. It just goes to show that money cannot buy love. I did not stay for the money because I had my own and I knew that money could not make me happy. In spite of it all, I think I stayed because I really loved him.

George just dropped out of life. He resigned his job, severed all friendships and remained at home till he took his last breath. There he purposed in his heart to give us the time of our life, cursing André and me daily as we took care of him. I don't think he even smiled once during the two years after surgery. What a waste of a very handsome and intelligent man! What in God's name happened to him when he was growing up? Background information is so very important. I did not have that and was completely lost as to what really happened to George. This must have been a generational curse that played out to its fullest. Only God knew the truth.

Finally, he died - a few weeks before my fiftieth
birthday. I was finally free.
Life was about to begin for me - at fifty.

Chapter Three

The quietness was loud in the house. Anderson was the first to break the uncomfortable silence. He was worried about my calmness and thought that I might explode.

"Mom," he said, and everyone lifted their heads as though he had called out to them.

"I cannot believe how well you're handling all of this. Are you sure you're okay?"

"I am fine, son," I replied, happy that the silence was over. I wanted to live.

"I expected it. Your father was ailing for two years. He did not die suddenly."

I saw the nods of agreement as I looked across the room. We were silent again for a short moment when Anton remembered the fun times we had at home in the early days. He started singing a familiar tune and the others joined in. Three tenors and a baritone, singing the ever popular "Amazing Grace". The church choir sang that song at almost everyone's funeral. It was not sung today though but I have four ex-choir members here and they sound like an entire choir. I had not heard them sing for so long. Oh, how I miss the years when they were teens! They grew up so fast. After one time is indeed another. The song ended and the moment was over much too quickly. Soon the voices were no more. Shortly afterwards, Anthony brought back to memory a lovely Negro spiritual medley and he started on that one. We all joined in, and for a while enjoyed what we had previously as a family. Oh the memories, I must ensure that we stick together. If I am not careful we will become a bunch of strangers.

This song, too, was over and they all sat again with smiles and chuckles that told me how much we missed each other, though it saddened me a bit knowing that it took a tragedy to bring us together again. We sat in the living room and chatted for another half hour or so, just enjoying each other's company. I then thought it a perfect time to remind them of what killed George and that they were all at risk. I started really calm: "You guys are well aware that your father died from various complications caused by prostate cancer, right? I have some stuff for you." I could almost hear their eyes following me to the little drawer on the coffee table where I placed the bottles.

"Here, one each. These are special vitamins for care of the prostate: saw palmetto and the works." I was careful to avoid their eyes as I handed them each a bottle. "By the way, did you get the test done? Did any of you go to see a doctor yet?"

The silence told me that that was a no. What is it with men? I asked them one by one the reason for not taking the test. Anton said that he refused to go to a male doctor and had not yet found a female physician that did the screening; Anthony said he was very busy and did not have the time; André too found himself too busy to bother and Anderson had to say something very flippant.

"Mom, I got the tests already. Actually, it was a lot of fun."

The looks he got made him cringe a little but I believe that he was just softening us up for the big announcement he had to make. I talked to them about how devastating prostate cancer was and made certain to remind them of the importance of knowing in the early stages. I literally begged them all to go take the test though. Well, as good sons, they promised their momma; but I'll just have to wait and see.

Anderson was waiting for his opportunity and suddenly stood up and said that he had an announcement. What came next was a blow that rocked my heart from its resting place.

"I am getting married!" he said, and waited expectantly for a reaction.

I swear my heart moved to the other side of my chest, making a pit stop in the centre; then returned to where it belonged. All of us were shocked and remained still, as if frozen in the spot. After what seemed like forever, André finally responded to what he thought was stupidity: "Man you tried that before. I still have the suit decorating my closet. Please, don't make the same mistake twice."

"This is not a mistake this time, Mom," Anderson insisted. "I am sure now and I won't turn back."

"How can you really be sure Anderson, do you even know how to please a woman?" asked Anton.

Anderson first hung his head, but then mustered up

the courage to inform us that he was not marrying a woman but a man. I think I fainted at this point. I knew a lot was going on but I could not contribute to their conversation. I was speechless. André and Anthony placed me on the couch and they were talking very loudly over my head. Something inside of me pulled me through because I had to say a thing or two to Anderson. I got up and I have no clue what happened to my tongue. I could not say a word. Maybe it was because his other brothers were handling that for me. Anderson kept defending himself and they argued back and forth for about ten minutes. I remained in a daze, refusing to believe that Anderson was serious about marrying a man.

Anthony's cell phone rang, interrupting the argument. I knew he had to go. He excused himself to take the call. There was a hush in the room; all I could do was look at Anderson in disbelief. He came up to me and held my hands.

"Mom," he began, "I cannot deny who I am anymore. I am a homosexual – my partner is a man. We are getting married but I will not embarrass you. We are eloping to where gay marriages are recognized. I am leaving in a few weeks. His name is Gerard and he is staying in a hotel in town. I am staying with him tonight. Mom... let me be me, okay!"

Somehow I could not even answer him; I held the tears back, but it took all my strength to do that. As Anderson picked up his belongings to leave, Anthony came in after talking on the phone.

"Where are you going? I need to talk to you."

"Let him go, Anthony. I'm done." I said, feeling like I had lost the battle.

After Anderson left, Anthony told us that the call he received was about a breakdown at the plant and he had to check it out. He too had to leave but promised to return to spend the rest of the weekend. We said our goodbyes as I tried to regain full consciousness by blocking the last hour from my mind.

After a while, Anton got up to get drinks for the three of us who had remained. He brought us each our favorite drink mix and I thought it was great that he remembered. André refused his, reminding Anton that he was now "saved and sanctified" so he did not partake of alcohol anymore.

"Come on, man," teased Anton, "You could drink five of these before you get tipsy far less for getting drunk." André was very sound in his faith though and simply rose and got himself a soft drink. We laughed and talked a little; then Anton said he had a 'hot date' and was leaving us soon as well. André thought he would pick him up on that because surely he was going out with someone he'd just met.

"Man, how can you sleep at night?"

"That's just it," Anton replied. "I don't sleep. I have more exciting things to do than sleep; unlike you who left the most beautiful woman I have ever seen, crediting that move to 'Jesus'. God made Eve because He said that man should not be alone."

André was quick on the draw, and responded with other scriptural references from the Bible.

"God also said that you shall not commit adultery, and that fornicators and adulterers will not inherit heaven. You live your life for earthly pleasures but I live mine for heavenly treasures."

Anton smiled craftily and sipped his drink; he just would not leave André alone.

"Why, are you waiting for Aphelia?" he asked.

"Do you really believe that she will come back here? People who go away to New York usually do not return to Trinidad. Come with me tonight. Natalie probably has a sister or a good friend. I'll call her."

"Not interested."

"Oh yes you are. You can't possibly give up sex because Aphelia is out of the picture. Come on, man; join me tonight."

Well I thought I had heard enough of my children talking about sex and broke into the conversation with a false cough, "Ahem."

"Sorry, mom," said Anton, as he got up and tidied himself to head out. "See you guys later."

André thought that he could have at least changed into something other than the clothes he had worn to the funeral. He looked at him with a peculiar crossed forehead and commented ...

"At least you can get out of those funeral clothes and take a shower."

"What for? Black is it, man. And what, you smell something?"

André just lifted his palms close to his head as if to say, 'I'm backing off.' Anton bade us farewell and headed for the door.

"Family breakfast meeting in the morning, Anton, so don't stay out all night."

"Okay, Mother, I hear you."

André and I remained in the living room and talked for a while longer. He was good with his brothers that day but I knew that something was bothering him. He never talked to me. This time I insisted. André complied, revealing how concerned he was about his brothers and their fate in life. I knew he was concerned, but that wasn't it, there was something else on his mind. However, I allowed him to talk about his brothers and did not trouble him with questions about Aphelia.

It seemed as though André was in my mind and reading my thoughts. I felt the same way he did concerning the boys. I could not help thinking: All my family members were prisoners! Anthony is a prisoner to his work as he blocked out a life with friends and family and got married to a job. Anton is a prisoner to sex, never committed to any relationship and I bet that he cannot count the number of women he has been with. Anderson is a prisoner to homosexuality. How can a man be in love with another man? Ooh, the thought made my blood crawl. And I myself was a prisoner to a mess of a marriage; being powerless against the abuse that I endured.

André was the only one who seemed to have his life mapped out. He was truly happy; actually I think the word is joyous. It seemed there was nothing on this earth that could make him as contented as he was. I knew he missed Aphelia and that situation saddened him a great deal but there was something that compensated for that loss. I really didn't want to say it because I do not believe in religious fanatics but I think that this "church thing" was really working for him. I was confused as to how he could be sad on one hand, yet happy on the other; unlike me who only pretended to be happy. It was so amazing.

I looked across at André sitting on the sofa sipping the soft drink, his mind a million light years away. Was this the right time? I wondered. What André did not know at that time was that Sonja and Aphelia had come to Trinidad for the funeral. They flew in a couple days prior to the ceremony and were visiting family in the country. She had called me to say that the car rental company could not furnish them with a car as promised and so she would take public transportation into town the next day. We planned then to go out for dinner.

As they had missed the funeral, André was still unaware that they were here. Sonja requested that I not say anything because Aphelia wanted to surprise André and to speak to him for herself. I was not really certain what it was all about but I just had a gut feeling that Aphelia wanted to make up with André. I believed with every drop of blood in my being that a reunion of those two love birds would be the happening of the century. He was so sad without her.

Their story is actually one of the most intriguing love stories ever told. Romeo and Juliet's hyped-up love affair which caused them both to die is no comparison with the love that André and Aphelia shared.

They had had a special friendship since they were kids. Actually it started before they even knew each other. Sonja and I were both pregnant that year. André was my third child but Aphelia was Sonja's first, and only. It was so bizarre. Neither of us really wanted to be pregnant.

This pregnancy was my third in as many years. Sonja unfortunately got pregnant after a one night stand. One of those stupid things you do at Carnival time. She hooked up with Lopez, a Spanish native from Venezuela who had come in for the Carnival season.

They spent a night together after a carnival cool down fete; he was due to leave the following day. They met that same day on Maracas Beach. She said they had talked all day long then she drove him to his hotel where she spent the night.

Before he left the following day, he gave Sonja all the remaining money he had and kept only enough TT currency for taxi fare and airport departure tax. She thought he was a sweetbread but she didn't know he had regarded her as a highly paid prostitute. After a night of sheer pleasure, he called a taxi and left for the airport. Sonja drove home. She did not think of possible implications. She did not know if she loved him or if he loved her. She did not even know his last name. Lopez had taken Sonja's phone number. She did not get his and he never called her.

A few weeks after Carnival that year, I was at home with my two toddlers at the time, Anthony and Anton, when Sonja came by to see me. I knew immediately that she was quite distressed about something. The fun-loving, smiling and blissfully cheerful woman I knew was replaced by a haggard and scared woman. She looked so horrible; I wanted to take her to a doctor. Before she could say a word the tears started rolling from her eyes in torrents, down her face and unto her soft silk blouse.

"My God!" I exclaimed. "What in the world is wrong with you? You look like you've seen the end of your life." I regretted saying that for a brief moment. I only hoped that she was not ill.

Sonja could not speak. She stretched out her hand and gave me a used, store-bought pregnancy test and I knew exactly what had happened. She had told me all about her rendezvous with Lopez and being my best friend, she would pretty much tell me everything; so I knew she was pregnant with the child of a stranger. I myself started to cry with her and hugged her so tight to my body that the beats of our hearts blended into one rhythm. I truly felt Sonja's pain that day.

André was already in my abdomen, just a few months older than Aphelia. As we hugged I felt like the children connected at that moment. I knew a little Bible so I tried to comfort Sonja by telling her that just like John jumped for joy in Elizabeth's womb when Mary who was pregnant with Jesus, came close to Elizabeth, I believe that our babies had just connected and they would be best friends. All Sonja could mutter between sobs was: "She ... will ...never ... know ... who ... her ... father ... is."

I have no idea if she really knew that it was a girl or if she just randomly called a gender. I already had two boys so I hoped that I too was having a girl. I held her even closer and promised her that we would take care of the baby together. Really I thought that these girls would be best friends; never imagining that our children would one day be not only best friends, but lovers.

Sonja got a hold of herself after a couple of weeks and made up her mind not to worry about the circumstances. André was born three months before Aphelia. When Aphelia came, Sonja spent the first few months of her maternity leave at my home and when she returned to work I kept Aphelia everyday with my kids for a while. Aphelia was about nine months when I had my fourth and last child, and so Sonja took her to the nursery to ease my burdens. I tied my tubes immediately after Anderson was born. I was just too fertile to leave myself open to another pregnancy; not to mention that I was really very tired.

Five years later, Sonja received a promotion coupled with an offer she could not refuse. The company offered her a position at their offices in New York. As kids we talked a lot about going to the Big Apple but I had to revise my dreams because now I had a husband and four kids. Sonja left Aphelia in the care of her grandmother who lived in the country and ventured to New York to work. She thought of leaving Aphelia with me but this was just about the time that George had started to abuse me so we both agreed that Aphelia would have to stay with her grandmother.

The new position offered her a lot of flexibility and she came home very often. I was a little envious but was also very happy for her. It was hard for me that she was away at this time in my life. I had no other friends as close as she was but I managed to live a very uppity life nevertheless. My acquaintances were working out just fine. None of them really knew my situation though. They thought I was married to the most wonderful man and expressed their jealousy of my relationship. If they only knew!

Sonja eventually took Aphelia to New York with her and she completed high school there. Aphelia became involved in so many extra curricula activities that Sonja's visits home became less and less frequent and after a few years we did not see her or Aphelia again anymore. She kept in contact by phone but it was more than ten years before she set foot back in Trinidad. Aphelia came back from time to time to visit her grandmother.

Many years later, André and Aphelia reconnected in a most astonishing way. That's why I believe that they were soul mates and neither could be happy without the other. One day the boys went on an excursion. They decided to go to Shark River, a very peaceful river on the road to Toco. On their way back from the outing, André noticed a vehicle partially hidden by some bushes a little distance from the road. As if fate had plotted their path, André was drawn to this vehicle and thought he should check it out. The others were in between opinions. Suddenly, André, who was driving, turned around sharply on the narrow country road and sped back towards the car in the bushes. His brothers thought he was crazy but André was at the wheel so they could do nothing - he was in control. André felt certain that he had a premonition; he just had to go back to see if anyone was hurt in the vehicle.

Upon reaching the spot where they had seen the vehicle, André stopped the car and jumped out as if he knew for certain that something was terribly wrong. The others followed him through the bushes to the car. What they saw was an extremely grievous site: the car had a single female occupant who was unconscious and slumped over the wheel. There were lacerations to her face and right shoulder and she was bleeding profusely. The window on the driver's side was smashed. It looked like a stone had been thrown at the car smashing the window and striking the driver. She was probably knocked out by the blow and the car veered to the left and into the bushes. A mound of sand and stones stopped the car from going over a precipice. There were no skid marks present which indicated that the driver was not speeding. If she had been, this accident would have been fatal.

Anton grabbed his cell phone to call for help – no service. The girl then moved a little and groaned in pain. André held her and carefully placed her head on his chest – that was when he realised that he knew who she was.

"Aphelia?"

"Uh, mmm," was all she could manage.

Anderson is trained in first aid and so he assessed her injuries and felt that they could move her safely and take her to a hospital themselves. Aphelia had come to Trinidad for a short holiday but it turned into a permanent move back home.

Growing up they knew each other like cousins but connected in a different way that night and he never left her side again until he became a Christian and broke up with her. I still cannot understand why he would do something like that.

Look at him now: the pain of not being with her is killing him. He has not so much as looked at anyone else since the break-up. Doesn't Jesus want us to be happy? Didn't God make us to want a companion? How can Jesus say to André that he should leave her? That was so confusing.

I wonder if I should tell him that Aphelia is here. No way! I really should not ruin the surprise. Sonja and Aphelia will both be here tomorrow. I thought, however, that I should just talk to my son. I really cannot bear to see him in so much pain: "André, why don't you just talk to me? You are obviously burdened. Do you miss your father?"

"I think I do miss him somewhat. I know he is Daddy, but ... I still haven't cried yet. Mom, what happened to us as a family? I saw a man lying on his dying bed for years and he was the meanest thing with the breath of life. He has no idea that I prayed for him every night after he fell asleep."

"You prayed for him every night?"

"Yep. I would go in there and place my hands on his

forehead and pray."

"Well, that never worked, did it?"

"The thing about God is that He forces no one to accept Him or the peace that He gives. He will prod our spirits but ... if you don't want it ... you don't want it."

He paused a little, still sipping the soda. He then turned to me: "This house is heavy. There is a spiritual blockage here and I cannot seem to peer through it. God has been showing me a lot of things"

"You see things, André?"

"I believe that I have the gift of the Word of Knowledge from God. Yes, I see things. I know you are strong Mom but what Daddy did to you is unimaginable."

I froze in my skin. Does he really know what happened between his father and me?

"Oh, Lord God. I don't really know You that well but please listen to me and honour my request. My kids cannot find out how horrible their father was. Please God, please."

I silently prayed this prayer before I asked him exactly what he knew: "What do you know about your father and me, André?"

"A lot more than you ever uttered. He abused you, didn't he"?

"For more than twenty years. Yes, he did. But what exactly do you know?

"I have no details, Mom. God is a gentleman. He will not embarrass anyone but He sent me back home to be with you."

"I think you are kinda crazy, but somehow I believe you."

"Yes, believe it. I had to move back here for the salvation of my family. I am only the vessel. I am not crazy though; I just want to obey Jesus."

André has the ability to soothe my fears each time we have one of our 'talks'. He is so wise; if I believed in reincarnation I would think he is wise King Solomon reincarnated. Knowing who I am and how I think, I would not listen to any of this religious mumbo jumbo from anyone. But there is something about my son - I do see a change in André. Something has happened to him on the inside; deep within his spirit. I am so afraid to delve into that arena; afraid of what I may find inside of me. Is this beast tamed yet? Maybe I should not try to find out ... not just yet.

"Well, before you get me converted tonight, let's change the subject. I noticed the expressions on your face when Anton teased you about not having a girlfriend. Tell me son, I want the whole truth, what really goes through your mind when you think about Aphelia?"

After a deep long sigh he began to pour his heart to me. I was shocked, but knowing what I now know – or thought I knew - I needed to hear this.

"I cannot hide my hurt from you, can I?

'Not a chance."

"I just chose not to talk about it. But I am broken in heart and soul; the pain I feel is indescribable. The most difficult thing I have ever had to do in my life was to break up with Aphelia. She is like an angel to me. What we had was so special I am convinced that I will never get it again. She came into my life as the perfect complement to my dreams and aspirations. I have seen her grow as well and I've witnessed her crossing rivers of success one after the other. Our lives became entwined with each other and we found out how to put two separate lives together as one. I really wanted to marry her; that was the only thing missing. As you know, we were shacked up, so according to God's standards we were living in sin. I prayed and prayed for a solution but God said, 'Not yet.'"

"You actually heard God speak, André?"

"I hear from God but I do not always hear a voice. I get this feeling that tells me the answers."

"But how can you be sure? How could God say no to that?"

"He did not say no; He said not yet. God is God and His ways are past finding out. In Isaiah 55:8, God says that our thoughts are not His and our ways are not His. He has a specific will for our lives and we live best when we conform to God's will."

"This does not sound right, André. It's as though God is holding out on you. God won't do something like that, would He?"

"I know it doesn't sound so clear and I myself was confused, hence the reason I disobeyed His commands. I did not understand why I could not be with Aphelia. We were already together for so long; so I thought I knew better than God did and asked her to marry me."

"You did? Well, what did she say?"

At that moment I seemed to have touched a really soft spot in André and the pain of losing Aphelia showed through as clear as distilled water.

"No! ... Mom, she said no."

And the tears flowed from his eyes. He was always so tough I did not know that he could cry. This is the first time that André had opened up to me concerning Aphelia. His answers to my questions were always short until then. I knew he was hurting but I did not know the severity of his pain. I walked over to the couch where he was and sat close to him. My son needed me and I was so happy that I could forget my own pain, even if it was just for a moment, and be there for him. I hugged him in an effort to comfort him. It was time for him to let it all out. We held each other for a few minutes then he managed to stop crying for a moment to continue his story.

"Aphelia had told me previously that she wanted to go back to spend some time in New York with her mother. She had also planned to complete her degree there as well. That was not just her plans, they were our plans. I had promised her that I would go with her, but then, God told me to stay here in Trinidad and I had to obey God."

"I do not fully understand the God thing. Everything else you've told me seems reasonable."

"I know, but I was certain of His instructions. Aphelia and I had another problem. She also felt like I wanted to marry her just so sex would not be a sin. She was very upset with me when I had stopped sleeping with her."

"You lived together, André. How could you take that from her?"

"That's the price I had to pay when I decided to follow Jesus. To worship God in spirit and in truth means that I cannot live in sin anymore. We all sin daily in thoughts words and deeds but to live in sin deliberately in that fashion was direct disobedience to God; 'insubordination' is probably a good word to explain it, and I just could not do it anymore."

"Well, she has always been a very understanding young lady..."

"Not on that topic. She refused to understand and really gave it to me that night. She had never raised her voice in such a loud manner before. I cannot get the image of her face out of my head. The hurt and pain she felt at that moment poured from her heart, then through her mouth. I think she knew what was coming next. She knew that I had to break up with her. I told her that she could still go to New York after we were married but she said she would not go as Mrs. Graham if I was not going with her".

I was very concerned about André but I felt as though I could not help him at all. He made me feel small; talking so grown up and with such wisdom. I just had to listen and shake my head and say "ah huh" and "mmm" at times, but André knew whose advice he was taking and was sold out to his God. He had this portion of scripture that he quoted on a regular basis: "Great peace have they that love Your law and nothing shall make them stumble" (Psalm 119:165). There was nothing I could say to him that would change his mind from this religious fanaticism. I must admit that it was working for him though. "Finding Jesus" had changed his life and I honestly loved what I saw. I let him continue to talk. He needed to get it off his chest; although I am sure he had already told God all about it.

"Mom, that was probably the first time that Aphelia was in so much pain and I could not comfort her. I tried to, but she refused to let me close to her. She cried half the night and did not go to work the next day. With a very heavy heart I left her at home and went to work. I thought it best to leave her alone. When I got home that day, she was gone. She had left her cell phone on my pillow. I knew that meant not to call her; I couldn't call her."

"You could have asked me for Sonja's number."

"No, I wanted to let her go free. I did not want to promise anything I could not deliver. I heard from her about one month later though. She sent a letter - there was no return address - but it was postmarked from New York. I got two more letters after that, then nothing. In the letters she told me that she was doing fine and that she missed me dearly and a lot of other things that made me believe that she would be back. I believe that God will direct her back to me one day. So for the past four years I just stayed close to Jesus and I know in my heart that she will be back. This is why I do not go out on dates. Remember, Mom, the tugging in my spirit was not an order not to marry her; I felt like God had said 'Yes, but not yet'".

I am very proud of André and the stance he took on his life. He is dogmatic. Nothing shakes him and nothing moves him; he is really firm in his belief. I can only hope now that my feelings about Aphelia's return are true. Did she really come back to him? Is this the time that André is anxiously awaiting; if all of this is true then there must be a God that lives in André and He must also be a mighty and powerful God!

I held back from telling André that Aphelia was back on the island. I have always let the kids live their own lives - from the time they all went out on their own - and only corrected them, as needed, if they asked. They will always know how I feel about their decisions but will never feel like I am making them do things that they don't want to. I like them to make choices for themselves and figure out the basis of their relationships on their own; be it co-workers, sports acquaintances or intimate relationships. They will learn from their own mistakes... and so will Anderson.

The telephone rang, disturbing my thoughts, and I rose to answer. Anderson was on the line. He had called to apologise for hurting me. I wondered how on earth he was going to fix that. I told him that it was his life and as long as he does not embarrass me nor his brothers all will be well. He asked me if he was still invited for breakfast. At first I hesitated but then I decided that he would always be my son, regardless. I made it quite clear though that I was not entertaining his friend. I got off the phone and went back to continue my conversation with André.

"That was Anderson on the phone"

"Oh yeah! What did he say?"

"He said he was sorry. I told him not to focus on it I know he knows how I feel."

"Mom, did you remind him about breakfast tomorrow morning?"

"He reminded me. But I made sure to say that he is to come alone."

Rufus began barking and fussing outside and we went out to the porch to see what was happening. It was Anthony. I was so happy that he was able to come back. On most occasions when he gets called away he is unable to return. Well, that's what he always says but I believe that he simply wanted to be alone. It is also my firm belief that Anthony never got over his father. Everybody else seemed to be okay but Anthony is in a shell. He had one girlfriend that I knew about. They broke up a long time ago and since then he never mentioned another. Maybe this weekend I'll get something out of him.

Anthony parked his car in the garage then decided to secure that part of the house before coming inside, Rufus was just making sure he was a welcomed guest. Anthony is always playing it safe; he would not leave his car parked on the street unless he had no choice. I had already sold George's car and the garage could hold two vehicles so Anthony called dibbs on that parking spot long before he had gotten here. The others didn't mind though.

He came home extremely tired and spent just a few short minutes with us downstairs before he retired to bed. André and I were getting ready to turn in as well; none of us would wait up for Anton since you can never tell what time he would come in. We talked for a little while longer and just as I was about to say good night, André asked me if I would like him to pray. Now, I like to hear him talk, but I can say my own prayers!

"How can someone think about Bible and prayer incessantly like you do? Isn't your life more than that?"

"Well, it is an extremely important part of my life, the most important actually."

"I know it is important but so is eating and nourishing our bodies; but we do not do it twenty-four/seven. Young man, you must learn to have some fun sometimes. God is pleased enough with the amount of wisdom and knowledge you poured out to me tonight. Nothing more, okay."

"Mom, you know what?"

"What?" I replied hoping that he would leave me be.

"I am a prisoner too. We all inevitably become prisoners to something or someone at some point in our lives. Sometimes we choose it and sometimes it chooses us. I choose to be a prisoner of Christ."

"Well, good for you, son. I choose to go to bed now. Good night, sleep tight; in the morning everything will be alright."

"Good night, Mom," replied André with a faint smile on his lips and much hope in his eyes. He reached out and hugged me once more as he planted a soft, but firm kiss on my cheeks. "I love you, Mom," he whispered, I then turned around and climbed the winding staircase and went to my room.

I went to bed but could not sleep. I was beginning to feel that tug in my heart again; I wanted to ignore it but it was way stronger than it ever was. André always made certain to discuss, even if it was for a short while, the essentials of living for Christ. Each time it would do something to me. This time I fought with all my might but it seemed as though he had planted an image of God in my head and I could not get it out. Maybe I should pray for a little while I thought; then knelt beside the bed and closed my eyes.

I tried to find words to tell God about some of my fears; nothing was coming to my head at all. Then I heard the piano. Apparently André did not go to his room right away for yet another night; instead he uncovered his piano and started to play and sing softly. André was a gifted musician and vocalist; he would sing songs that the great singers had recorded but he had also composed a few of his own. I think he needs a promoter though. This Graham tenor can measure up to Pavarotti any day! As he played and sang softly, the melodious music made its way up the staircase and into my room. It provided a comfort to my weary soul. I did not need to think about words to pray anymore; the song said it all for me. André was singing Billy and Sarah Gaines' popular, "A Friend Indeed". The words of this song were prophetically soothing...

> *Somebody here has a broken heart*
> *Somebody's gonna cry when they're all alone*
> *Somebody here just does not quite yet understand*
> *That Jesus died to bear*
> *Every single care that we have*

> *CHORUS*
> *There's no heartache there's no pain*
> *That He cannot feel not a wounded spirit He cannot heal*
> *No burden too big to bear, or load He won't share*
> *Cause in our need, yes, He's a friend indeed*

> *Somebody here has a question now*
> *Wondering if others ever hurt this way*
> *Somebody's dying just to know that Jesus hears*
> *Every single groan And He will never leave you alone*

> *There's no heartache there's no pain*
> *That He cannot feel Not a wounded spirit He cannot heal*
> *No burden too big to bear, or load He won't share*
> *Cause in our need, yes, He's a friend indeed*

> *He sees, He feels, He knows every heartache we endure*
> *And for each of life's woes I know, I know that Jesus is the cure,*
> *He is the cure*

> *There's no heartache there's no pain*
> *That He cannot feel; not a wounded spirit He cannot heal*
> *No burden too big to bear, or load He won't share*
> *Cause in our need, yes, He's a friend indeed.*

Tonight, like many other nights, I am once again comforted by a song, but I still cannot comprehend the mystery. I am getting closer and closer to finding out what is making such a difference in André's life. He probably had no idea that I actually stayed awake almost every night listening to him sing and praise and give God thanks. He really does not thank God for anything in particular. I hear him say things like, "I worship You, Lord, just because of who You are"; "You are God all by Yourself". Is God that real? I wonder; but then I think that God is actually charmed by the attention that André bestows on Him, because I could have felt the very atmosphere in the house shift. This has got to be a relationship! It has nothing to do with religion. It is different!

Just as I thought he was finished I heard a lovely tune, one that I had never heard before.

God You know I'm trying to live holy
God You know I'm trying to live right
I am just a man and I know that I'm not perfect
I have to depend on You and so You give me Strength
That's why I choose to be a Prisoner of Christ
I choose to be bound by Your love,
and chained in Your Might
In You, O Lord, I find Life and Joy and Peace
And though I am a Prisoner, I am Free

God I know I have been captured by Your love.
I gave up all worldly pleasures and now look to things
from above
I am no longer bound in sin and I'm not ashamed
Cause I've been washed in Your blood
and now freely call Your Name

That's why I choose to be a Prisoner of Christ
I choose to be bound by Your love,
and chained in Your Might
In You, O Lord, I find Life and Joy and Peace
And though I am a Prisoner, I am Free

I am a Prisoner of Christ,
Not bound with chains of steel
A Prisoner of Christ, bound by a love that is so real
I'm a Prisoner 'cause He died to set me free
Though I am a prisoner, I am Free

When I asked about this song, he revealed that he had written it; but when did he write this song, I wondered? The words were so indicative of the standpoint he had taken on life. We spoke about it earlier that night. 'We are all imprisoned, either by someone or something throughout the course of our lives'. He had willingly become a prisoner of Christ. He made the choice – he chose this prison. Freely giving up your own life to Christ to do His will, is certainly the best type of prisoner to be.

Chapter Four

KNOCK! KNOCK! BANG! BANG!

𝔄 very loud knocking woke me up. The sun glared through the thin blinds of my bedroom window. I could not recall the last time that the sun beat me to rising in the morning. I have watched the sun come up every day for as long as I could remember. André was already up and he was the first to open his door and run downstairs. I heard the voices and I knew that Anderson had arrived for breakfast. The first thought in my mind was to do something to knock the brains back into his head. But, having just enjoyed the most peaceful night I had had in years, I had to scotch that idea.

'Just smile, Mel, and talk pleasantly to your son,' I counseled myself, remembering that Sonja was scheduled to arrive that morning. I decided that I would enjoy what was promising to be a beautiful day and I was going to refuse to let Anderson or anything else mess up my mood.

I really didn't want to get up but I had to though. I promised the boys to prepare a breakfast like I used to when they were kids.

"Come on, come on, Melinda, pull yourself together," I commanded myself.

I then sort of rolled from one side to the other, lifted myself up and glided over to the windows and opened them. The fresh morning breeze rushed in and filled my room. I closed my eyes as the breeze rushed past my face. It brought with it a remembrance of the pleasant conversation I had with André the night before. It was as though God himself was breathing His Words into my life. My spirit was beginning to be awakened by the strong presence of a caring being; it must be God.

I knew I wanted to know Him but I just didn't think I needed to talk about Him all the time as André did. I had made up my mind, however, to be a little open. I would start going to church at least once a week; not two and three times as André did. He bought me a Bible and I promised to read it every morning, just not that morning. I reminded myself that I had to get ready to go downstairs. All would be well I guess, as long as I thought about Jesus a few minutes each day. He must be pretty busy anyhow. André alone talked to Him all the time.

As I entered the kitchen I was surprised that Anderson, André and Anthony were already well on their way to preparing the breakfast.

"Good morning, guys. I was supposed to do that."

"The worms are beginning to eat my intestines, Mom," replied Anderson, as he came up to me and gave me a big hug. "We could not wait any longer. I, for one, am starved!"

"Where is Anton?" I asked as I noticed there was no indication that he was even home.

"I don't know," said Anthony. "I did not see him. Maybe he did not sleep here last night."

André knew that Anton did sleep at home; he also knew that Anton did not sleep at home alone. He said nothing, but was very concerned about the implications if Anton was not able to slip the girl out before I found out.

"No, no, he slept here last night; he came in very late though," he confirmed.

Anderson and I began setting the large dining table that had not been used for a very long time. I made sure to dust and polish it quite frequently so that it would retain its beauty. It was an oval shaped table made of solid teak. I had it specially made, having a 'thing' for dining rooms. Yes I do. If families intend to stay together, I believe that the dining room should be the most used room in the house, and so I tried to create such a room. That table cost a pretty penny and had the potential to outlive all of us. It was a fine investment and an antique, worth now at least three times its original cost. It is sad that it did not fulfill its purpose for my family; at least, up to this point.

As we were finishing up with the table, we thought that we heard voices upstairs and went to investigate. Walking towards the stairway we saw Anton coming and I almost dropped when I saw a female companion. She was scantily dressed-the denim skirt barely covering her buttocks. The rage in me was fierce but I managed to hold my tongue. Anton thought it was a good idea to introduce her to me; in fact, it was really a good mistake!

"Mom, this is Princess."

"I could not care less if she is Queen Elizabeth," I

thundered, "What is she doing in my house? And weren't you supposed to go out with Natalie last night?"

The young woman cringed a bit but was a little hot pepper herself. Imagine she actually opened her mouth and replied: "I was invited by Ancil. I did not scale the fence." She spoke in a most annoying 'child-who-grew-up-too-fast' voice.

"His name is Anton! What kind of woman are you that you come into a house with a man whose name you don't even know? Didn't your mother teach you anything?"

I was getting into her face by that time and André and Anthony, who had come into the dining room after hearing loud voices, had to step in between us. André especially wanted to protect my heart from anything that would hinder the work that God was doing in there. Anthony was just mad as to how insensitive Anton could be and the level of disrespect he demonstrated.

"Come on, Mom," said Anton. "I am a big man now. What are you fussing about?"

"These types of illicit activities should be undertaken in your own home, not mine!"

"So what you saying, I have no rights here?"

"Listen! First, get this prostitute out of my house, then we could talk mother to son?"

The girl became highly upset when I referred to her as a prostitute and she tried to defend herself, I refused however to allow her to speak in my house. I had seen enough of these little girls come into my life and my marriage and I had to pay for their indiscretion. They do whatever they want to get money and don't have an ounce of care for the women that they hurt. I had hoped that Anton was not like his father but that day I saw that he probably inherited the gene. He had the same attitude. Princess could not be more than eighteen; legally of age but so stupid. Anton realised that there was nothing he could say that would make me simmer down and so he just turned and decided to obey my instructions.

"Princess, let me just take you home. I'll buy you breakfast."

"Good idea. I really don't need these insults at all."

She wanted to be as rude as she possibly could, so she spun around sharply and something dropped from the jacket she had folded over her arm.

"Is this my wallet, Princess?" said Anton, as he reached for it in astonishment.

"Well, I told you that I was behind on my rent and I wasn't sure if you would pay it …"

"Just get out!" yelled Anton, realizing what a fool he had been.

Princess had already hardened her heart and soul, and was in such a state, that insults like those did not really bother her at all. She simply turned and went out the front door, closing it behind her with a great big slam. We looked at her leave but then, all of a sudden, I felt different. The event left a little hole in my own heart. I actually felt like there was something in me that could have helped her, but - how could that be? Girls like that made me upset; they awaken all the hurt, pain and suffering that I had endured at George's hand. How could I be of help to her? What a strange feeling for me because I could barely stand the sight of her. I almost did not consider her human. Help her! No way!

As I pondered on those things, Anton had been going through his wallet to make sure that everything was there. Thankfully, nothing was missing. He sat quietly, deep in thought. He really did not want to be like this at all, but why was it so hard to stop? My anger began to subside because I realised that Anton needed help. Instead of blowing my top at him I asked the others to give us a moment. It was time for a heart to heart talk with Anton. His attitude towards women and relationships was definitely not good and God alone knew what that could lead to.

"Son, what is happening to you?"

"I am out of control, Mom. It is as though someone has tied a rope around my neck and constantly tugs at me. The rope tightens with each tug, forcing me to commit these acts."

I heard George's voice and George's reasoning and I hated the thought that I had raised a George. I wanted to scream but once again I had to be strong. I believed that if I told him about his father he would give it up. But on the other hand, he could think that he inherited this atrocious behaviour and could do nothing about it. I did not want to give him a reason to continue so I held my tongue.

"I know you can break this, Anton."

"Mom, I want to break it. I have tried but I can't. I don't know what to do."

"This is not just only a grievous sin against God. These actions can take you down a path of destruction."

"I know. My funds are almost completely depleted."

"Anton, are you broke?" He shook his head. "Give me all

the credit cards."

"Mother?"

"Yes, give them to me, right now!" He took all four credit cards and gave them to me. I could see the humiliation on his face. He was a "big man" yet I was doing this to him.

"And the bank card, please." He complied without a single word of protest, but wondered how he would live.

"Mom, what am I going to do for money?"

"We'll talk about that tomorrow when I come up with a plan."

"You are going to ask me to go talk to someone right."

"Wow! You are my son, so smart. You need help and I will get help."

He nodded his head in agreement. We then joined the others in the dining room. His brothers were still very angry but when they saw my calm they backed off. Breakfast was ready by then and we sat to have the first breakfast together in the house in more than ten years.

I smiled as I saw my boys grab for the eggs, pancakes and hash brown that they themselves had prepared and I thought, "They are fine cooks. I raised them well". I could not eat just yet - I just sat there and stared at them one by one, fixing their problems in my head. I did have four fine sons though. No one is perfect, so I guess I had to accept the imperfections in each one of them and just try to enjoy them. I wished that the visit could last much longer but they all had their lives and would be leaving in a couple of days.

Anthony invaded my thoughts with a question that I really wanted to deal with later on: "What's on the agenda today, Mom?"

'Oh, boy! Here it comes,' I thought. Now André would know that Aunty Sonja is here. I fumbled a little and wondered if I had given away the secret: "Um, actually Sonja is here."

André dropped his fork and raised his head. He glared at me and I knew what he was thinking, but he did not say anything.

"We are going out to dinner tonight. As a matter of fact, we can all go out to dinner tonight. She will be here by lunch time."

I hoped that André would not ask me anything because I did not want to lie to him and I also did not want to reveal Aphelia's secret. Anton, on the other hand is a wicked soul. Before André could even ask the question I saw in his eyes, Anton began to tease him relentlessly. All André would say as he smiled at me was: "Who laughs last laughs best, bro. Who laughs last laughs best." I knew he knew. He said that he had a feeling that Aphelia would come back to him but I tried my best to ignore his gaze because I knew I would answer the question without saying a word. I would be extremely happy if the reason she wants to see him is what he wants to hear.

I then asked the boys if they had anything planned for later and if not they should come to dinner with us. Anthony was still very tired and it showed. He seemed so far away most times, always 'working away from work'; sorting out work issues, sometimes on the laptop but most times just in his head; he promised to go though. Anton really could not risk another episode like earlier that morning. He surely was not going out to look for girls that night. He had no money either so he was not remaining at home, no doubt. André I know for sure had no plans and I know he would go without our even asking. Anderson on the other hand said he could not make it because he had other plans. No one asked him for details. I then asked André to make bookings at the newly opened restaurant in Central that we had heard so much about.

We finished up breakfast, cleaned up the kitchen and planned to spend the rest of the morning quietly.

I could hardly wait for Sonja's arrival. I had not seen her in years and wondered what she looked like. However Sonja's appearance was really the least of my anxiety. I was a lot more anxious about Aphelia and André seeing each other again after such a long time. Would he propose to her again and if so would she say yes? I didn't know if he could handle any rejection right now. I was getting really nervous as well because André was actually waiting for her to return and was adamant that she would come back to him. It was now only a matter of time.

Michelle Paula Barton-Romeo

Chapter Five

That day after the funeral was the longest day of my life. God must have extended the hours just so he could put things in perspective for me. It seemed like everything that needed to happen to set me on course did. I sat on the porch awaiting Sonja's and Aphelia's arrival. She had called when they were just about to leave their family's house in Toco. The boys were washing their cars and playing water games. Weren't they too old for that? However, they were having a lot of fun and I was enjoying looking at them.

Some of the neighbours peeped through their windows. They had not seen a scene like this in years. A few of them came over to say hi to the boys. Oh these stupid nosy fools! I know how they think; they would want us to stay indoors and mourn for George, clueless to the fact that we have been mourning all along while he was still alive. For God's sake, two years ago the doctors gave him nine months – how much longer should he live in that state anyway? Not a single one of them came over to see how he was doing - these high-society, puffed up, pretentious people, so rich and stupid. I often wondered how many of them were truly happy. Most are fairly new neighbours. The former ones all sold their homes to these snobs who wanted to live in the city. We never got too close to them at all. They didn't want us to, anyway. I was glad, too, because my life had been a big secret.

The chuckles from these boys broke my concentration. They were like kids, laughing, running, and playing. The yard was once again alive with the sound of kid-like fun. I was so enjoying my sons; and what was even better was that they were enjoying themselves. Anthony especially brought joy to my heart because I don't think I saw him laugh since he had arrived on Thursday night. One by one they returned indoors to dry themselves and get ready for lunch. We were having coconut bake and saltfish buljol with sorrel and ginger beer, in picnic style on the lawn, in the back yard. That was Anton's idea; had to be him, the player. He must have tried that so many times to entice his girlfriends.

Suddenly, I missed our dog. "Where is Rufus?" I asked. The gate was open and I thought he had run away. Anton went down the road to find him but he was nowhere to be seen. "Maybe he will come back later," I said, then slumped back into my chair.

I stayed on the porch and waited excitedly for my friend; it was as though I was expecting my significant other. However, Sonja can be described as an extra special person in my life and I had not seen her in over ten years. I knew, however, that most of my enthusiasm was concerning Aphelia. Just as I began reminiscing, the taxi pulled up outside our house. It was then I realised how much I missed my dear friend. I knew the feeling was mutual. I started down the driveway and Sonja started up; we met almost in the middle and I cried like a baby as she wrapped her arms around me. We screamed like we were sixteen-year-old school girls again. I was delighted to see her. In that moment Sonja had forgotten all about Aphelia who was left with the baggage and the driver. She came into the front yard, her regular, pretty little sassy self: "Don't mind me, Aunt Mel; I'm fine, I'll manage…"

I had to literally push away from Sonja to grab a hold of this precious girl.

"Come here! Gimme a hug, child. You look fabulous."

Anthony and Anderson were getting lunch ready and heard the commotion. They came outside, their jaws dropping in astonishment on seeing Aphelia but obviously wanting to be sensitive to André who was on his way outside as well. Anton then came out with André who froze when he laid his eyes on her. Anton greeted them, and as usual had something smart to say.

"Girl! You are even more beautiful than when I last saw you. Are you sure you're the Aphelia we know?"

"Yes I am and tell me something I don't know," she replied with her typical sassiness.

"Wow! But I know you don't want to see me."

He turned around and noticed that André had not moved from the spot.

"Unfreeze, André. Come on!"

That moment was like a scene from a romance movie. They looked at each other and every one of us knew exactly what was happening. He slowly walked towards her and she did not move. I was certain that I saw her heart pounding through her chest. That was the first time I saw the length of her lovely hair – she had straightened it and it hung loosely around her shoulders; the gentle breeze made it swing just a tad. She could not have chosen a nicer outfit for this occasion. She looked absolutely gorgeous in a blue and white wrap dress with capped sleeves and frills accentuating the hem line and along the front. She wore white three inch high slippers that showed off her recently pedicured feet and nicely polished toes. Her make-up only enhanced her beauty - no harsh colours – everything blended well into the tone of her skin. She is really a lovely young lady. My other sons had to be happy for André. She was taken.

It seemed like forever before he reached the spot where she stood; but they had not taken their eyes off of each other. The look in her eyes answered all his questions and his eyes answered all hers. André placed his arms around Aphelia like he was holding his future and simultaneously securing its treasures. The two shared a moment together as they blocked everyone else out of the little world that their love had created. I think my questions and concerns were also answered. They returned to earth shortly afterwards and released each other. Talk about non-verbal communication. Wow!

We gathered in the back yard for our picnic. I really did not want that moment to end. What with all these familiar voices and familiar faces. The picnic lasted for about two hours. We spent the time catching up on things we had missed out on over the years. The rainy season was approaching though and a shower made us continue our little party indoors.

Sonja and Aphelia had decided to stay with us for the remainder of their trip. We excused ourselves and went to get settled in while the boys took care of the lunch wares and the kitchen.

The entire mood of that day was so refreshing. I felt free and easy. Only God could have made possible the gaiety among us. I had been yearning for that. I would have done anything to have a loving atmosphere in our lives consistently. George - he had spoiled everything! Maybe I did have a chance to get my life back, to get my kids back. I purposed to find the way; I thought there must be one.

Aphelia left us and went downstairs. She and André then disappeared; no doubt they had a lot to talk about. Anderson went back to his hotel room, Anthony to his computer and Anton fell asleep on the sofa. Sonja and I practically had the entire house to ourselves. We laughed, cried, screamed, and simply enjoyed each other's company. Soon however it showed that we were no longer teenagers and fell asleep on the plush rug in my room.

Aphelia woke us up around six o'clock and reminded us that we had dinner reservations for 7:30 p.m. We had decided to go to Enterprise village in Central for dinner and so had to leave Woodbrook by 6:45 p.m. We were then in somewhat of a rush to get dressed. I called out to André to fasten my necklace for me and the look on his face when he came in was one to die for.

"Don't ask, Mom. We'll talk about it later. But you knew she was here, didn't you? "

"Yes I did, but she had specific instructions and I really did not want to spoil it. Please, tell me, I'm dying to know."

"She is not going back to New York with Aunty Sonja."

I was elated to hear that but I know that it did not automatically mean that they would have rekindled the relationship; so I wanted to hear more.

"Oh my God, does this mean what I think it does?"

"Well, she told me enough to believe that it will happen."

"I am so happy for you, André."

"I am happy for me. Now let's go or we'll be late."

By then it was 7:00 p.m. and the stretch limousine had been waiting outside since 6:30. My sons decided to rent the limo so we could ride together in one vehicle. Sonja realised that Anderson was missing and asked if we were picking him up at the hotel. I just squeezed her arm and she knew I meant not to ask about him then.

We were heading to the luxurious "Le Paridis Magique", French for The Magical Heavens. This restaurant was André's choice because they did not play any lewd music nor was it loud like a fete. Rather, it featured a more family friendly atmosphere and their genre was basically ballads, rhythm and blues, and gospel. They also did not serve alcohol. Although we had heard a lot about this fabulous place, it was our first visit.

The limousine ride was smooth and comfortable. Really, that day could not be any more perfect. Anthony and André looked fantastic in their suits. I had not had the opportunity to see them dressed up for a long time; at least not since Anderson's aborted wedding. I was accustomed to seeing André because he always dresses up. Aphelia looked stunning, like an angel from heaven. André's eyes lit up as they whispered to each other from time to time. A little part of me was feeling a bit guilty as it was only the day before that we had buried George. Should I pretend to grieve? No way! I really was grieving a little but as I always say, there is nothing I can do for those who have passed on but I can do a lot for the rest of us who are alive and those I would like to maintain meaningful relationships with. My family needed that! George had alienated every one of us; I had the chance to change the situation. I could not care less that George's death was bringing me happiness. I needed my sons more than ever.

The limousine stopped, jolting me back to the moment at hand. I was out of the limo first and smiled a huge smile as my family members exited, one by one. Oh, how I missed them; I wished the night would never end. We occupied a huge table in the centre of the restaurant. The other patrons were probably wondering who we were but that night everyone else was invisible for me. No one mattered at the moment. Afterwards we would quit being self-absorbed but that night belonged to us.

The meal was sumptuous. I did not pay attention to what each one chose for the main course but we all had the house soup for the appetizer. They served a local soup made with dasheen leaves, pumpkin, carrots, and corn. It was well-prepared and was very tasty, a true appetizer.

We had a wonderful time during dinner. The background music was really soothing, André and Aphelia lit up when they heard a song that brought back memories for them. I was amazed at their openness when they shared a little with us. They then got up to dance, we watched them as they approached the dance floor. Anton stared as though he was thinking a little about his own life. Anthony was also amazed and extremely happy for André. As I looked at Aphelia, what I saw was a woman who could love no other. How did she manage being separated from André for four years?

"I have never had anything like that," Anton finally confessed as he watched their every move.

"I cannot begin to understand why they broke up in the

first place," Anthony added. "Mom, André is really changed you know. I think Aphelia will love him even more than before." It was obvious to all of us that they were truly made for each other. I had heard a theory about "soul ties". If I believed it, this was a very good example.

I thought that André would have forgotten how to dance as he had stopped going to parties, but I was wrong. He moved around the dance floor like a professional. They danced a couple of songs without taking a break. I was certain that I saw a hint of jealousy on Anton's face. I knew I was correct when he repeated André's comment that was said at the breakfast table: "Well, who laughs last really laughs best." Anthony and Anton then went to the bar to get drinks. Sonja and I sat alone at the table nibbling the cheese cake we had ordered for desert.

"You really think we should be eating this?" Sonja asked as she placed a huge portion in her mouth.

"Well I hope you can chew," I replied mischievously. We laughed and talked a little, then Sonja became serious.

"Melinda," she called my name in full when she needed my attention. "I have something to tell you."

I got a little worried and my mind thought a million thoughts all at once. Sonja could always tell when I got concerned and she immediately calmed my fears.

"Hey, girlfriend, it's nothing bad; serious, but not bad."

"Whew, I really cannot handle any more bad news."

"I am a Christian now. I got saved a few years ago."

"How come you never told me?"

"I don't know, figuring out things, I guess. I have found out though that the Jesus André talks about is real."

"I know Jesus is real, but don't you think that it is all hyped up too much. He behaves so over-enthusiastic most times. Other than that I like it."

"Look at them," she said using her head to point in the direction of André and Aphelia who was still dancing. "Aphelia got saved too."

I was very excited to hear that because I know it would make all the difference in their relationship; André's salvation being the reason for the breakup in the first place.

"You're kidding me!" I exclaimed.

"Nope, believe it. She had been waiting for this day for a while now."

"Sonja, you know what this means. Why didn't she come back sooner?"

"God has His way of doing things ..."

"Yeah, yeah, André tells me all the time. Look, I like what I see in André, it has changed him - I am happy for him and I am honestly happy for you and Aphelia too. I would like to experience some of it – but not all – it's too much."

Sonja backed off a bit telling herself that as long I was willing to acquire a little, God would do the rest. We ordered wine and watched the boys on the dance floor. Anthony and Anton had joined André as the music changed. It was really nice and they were enjoying every minute of it.

"Isn't it great they all can have fun together? André's

faith prevents him from hanging out with them at clubs and bars, that's why he chose the place."

"Yeah it's ...." Sonja paused as though she had seen a familiar face.

"Isn't that Harold over there?"

I looked across; it surely looked like him.

"Well I think so, but, what is he doing all the way down here? Is he working here?"

"Looks that way. Let's call him over, Mel."

"Please, don't do that! Ooooh, he's still so cute!"

"You guys really liked each other back then."

"Yep, but I really couldn't have an extramarital relationship."

"I think he saw us."

"Really?"

"Oh, stop acting like a baby. You should hook up with him again if he's still single."

"Sonja, I just buried my husband."

"No. No. No. You buried him a long time ago. You only put the body in the ground yesterday."

Maybe Sonja was right about that but I had a little pride in myself and besides, I didn't know if I wanted a man in my life at all. I felt devoid of love – I would simply hurt anyone who came into my life. Don't even mention intimacy – George had turned sex into an evil experience. That part of me was dead, I was sure of it. But Harold was definitely coming over to the table so I had to smile and clear my mind.

"As I live and breathe," he said as he reached out and kissed us both.

"Melinda, Sonja, I would have never thought! It's been a very long time."

We both smiled and exchanged greetings while I wondered how he was able to remain so good looking and muscular after all these years.

"Now which one of you is celebrating her sixteenth birthday? You guys look magnificent!"

Harold was always quite charming. He was still standing so I invited him to sit with us for a while. Sonja kept that look in her eyes as we conversed. We remembered the times when we sang at the restaurant he managed in Port-of-Spain. Harold told us that managing that restaurant had stirred up his interest in the industry and when this one went into receivership he bought it. He changed the name and upgraded the ambience and now he was really enjoying the fruits of his labour.

"Well congratulations are in order," I said, thinking that he turned out a lot better than I did.

"Thank you, Melinda, but what happened to you? It's like you fell off the face of the earth."

"Well," I replied, thinking of what I should say, "actually George got pretty ill and as a matter of fact, we buried him yesterday."

"Oh my, I'm so sorry. I had no idea."

"He was ailing for a very long time. He is no longer in pain now." In my heart I completed what I really wanted to say 'and I am in no pain either'.

"I do hope that you enjoyed the dinner."

"We did," we replied, almost in unison.

"Great! Well ladies, the next round of drinks are on the house." He signaled for a waitress.

"Please get them whatever they want okay, no charge. I need to go and check some stuff in the kitchen. Are you leaving soon?"

"Ye..." I started but Sonja beat me to it.

"No!" said Sonja. "Our grown kids are also here and they do not want to leave now at all. Just look at them."

Anton and Anthony had made friends with other people at the bar. There was a huge group over there engaged in conversation, so they looked like they were really having a time. André and Aphelia was still in their own little world.

"I will be back in five," Harold said as he walked to the kitchen area.

The waitress took our orders and went to prepare them. Sonja looked at me with a slight smirk. I tried to avoid her but she could be so persistent.

"What?" I asked with a mixture of exclamation and curiosity.

"What do you mean, "What?" What do you think?"

"I don't know what to think. Girl, I need to breathe."

"Hey look, he is talking to his staff, doing his job I guess - but staring at you, Mel. Look, 3'oclock."

I did not really want to look but I wanted to see if he was really looking at me, showing interest in me. I had been locked away with George for so long that I did not think of another person in that way at all – except Harold, years ago. I glanced across. He smiled and twiddled his fingers in a wave. I smiled back. I did like it but Sonja liked it more than I did. I wished she would leave me alone.

"You guys should sing one of the ballads that you used to sing when he worked at Anne's Restaurant."

"Girl, please. I have not sung anything in years. I'll probably croak like a frog."

"No, you won't. As soon as he comes back I'm going to suggest it to him."

"You will do no such thing. Let me grieve in peace."

"Don't pull that one on me. Grieve, yeah right."

Harold came back to the table while we were talking and although I gave her the eye, she still suggested that we sing. Harold was excited and thought that it was a great idea. We did sing a lot at our longtime favorite place, Anne's Restaurant. Singing used to take my mind off the situation with George. I remembered that I used to pretend that Harold was my husband so when we sang love songs I would sing it for real and 'wow' the audience. I didn't think I could pull that off again. But Harold and Sonja were certain that I could. I gave in and we went to the stage. The lights in the restaurant were turned a little lower; the spotlight was on us and the music began. He chose the ever popular "Endless Love" by Diana Ross and Lionel Richie. I was surprised that I felt so comfortable up there. Harold had introduced us the way we used to be which was a bit of a shock to the boys because they did not know that I used to sing at the restaurant; they had thought I only worked there. As we sang I was not even there at all, my mind wandered all over my past.

Harold dedicated the song to all the couples and invited them to the floor. Most of them obliged as we started to sing. About half way through the song, something strange happened: everyone stepped aside slowly encircling André and Aphelia who were front and centre. André was on his knees and Aphelia had her left hand stretched out to him and her right hand covering her mouth. There was silence, except for the blend of our voices as we continued to sing in acappella as even the musicians stopped playing. By this time everyone knew what the question was and they also knew her answer. I could hardly believe my eyes and was delighted that I was actually serenading my son and soon to be daughter-in-law.

After he placed the ring on her finger, he rose to his feet; their eyes fixated on each other. He gently pulled her towards him and accompanied by thunderous applause from the onlookers, he lightly pecked her lips with his. The musicians resumed playing and as we continued, they hugged each other. André lifted his gaze to the stage and winked at me. I could see his joy. I knew he had waited for her but had no idea that he also had a ring waiting. Aphelia was pleasantly surprised and savoured the moment. She was the centre of attention and I think she deserved it. They danced alone as we finished the song while the circle of strangers applauded them to the end.

We then all gathered at the table. By that time I was really in awe thinking that this night could not get any better. Harold brought us a bottle of champagne and we celebrated with them and had a few more laughs.

No one asked about Anderson at all. He had made his choice. We were sorry, but there was no way I would let him bring a man along with us. He seemed normal so I could not understand why he chose to be with Gerard when there was a family gathering. However, I decided not to be stressed over it. One day Anderson would realise that this way of life was contrary and he would turn around and conform to the natural and Godly purpose of human sexuality.

As I was pondering on this very subject you can guess who walked up to our table. Yes, my son, Anderson. I would have smiled except that he had come with a man. I know if he only called him Gerard, I would kill him. I was really nervous, though he was smiling, I could not smile. He greeted us all, then introduced his friend: "This is Gerard."

I could hardly believe my ears. I rose to my feet. There was a hush, the rest of the family wondering what I would do. I could have taken him out right there and then. My eyes filled up with tears – I was so angry that he had showed up with that freak. I then became even angrier because he made me cry. "How dare you!" I bellowed. Everyone thought I was talking to Andy but I was speaking to Gerard. I knew that I could not blame him but I was going to anyway: "How dare you come in here with my son? You are a poor excuse for a man. What the hell are you encouraging him to do?"

There was silence in the entire restaurant as my voice rose above the music. Anderson thought I was really out of place and so he tried to quiet things down.

"Mom, you're making a scene," he said, looking like I had embarrassed him so badly he could sink into the ground.

"You are ashamed of my outburst but not ashamed of

yourself, claiming to love a man. You are a man!"

"Mom, please!" he begged but I wouldn't hear him.

I tore into Gerard as if he had held a knife to Andy's throat and had forced him to be homosexual. Honestly, this is what I wanted to say to Andy but I never got the chance so I gave it to Gerard instead.

"You are just plain nasty!" I continued. "God should never allow you guys to live."

André then grabbed hold of me and literally pulled me aside. He whispered to me that this was really not the way to handle the situation. Sonja apologised to Harold on my behalf and we left the restaurant. I was inconsolable, uncontrollable, and mad as hell. Gerard came up to me and tried to talk. He should not have done that; now I was enraged to the highest point.

"Mrs. Graham, I really love him."

"Do you even know what love is? Did someone hit you with a stupid stick? Have you any idea why God destroyed Sodom and Gomorrah. He hates your kind. You stink! Be careful boy; fire may fall on you even as we speak."

Anderson decided that he had had enough of the mess; he held Gerard's arm and tried to pull him away. "Gerard, let's just go. Okay!" his voice quivering as he was a little unable to hide how he felt about my conduct.

"Let go of me wimp!" yelled Gerard, as he spun around wildly making a fist with his hand. "I can handle myself."

Andy threw his hands up towards his face as if to block a blow; he was cowering in fear. There it was, my worst fears were confirmed: Anderson was being abused by this man. There was fright in his eyes - a look of sheer terror. A mother must never be placed in such a position. It hurt so badly to see that he was the weaker one in the relationship; he was helpless, I was helpless. His brothers stared in disbelief while Sonja held on to me. It was unbelievable; what had become of Andy was unbelievable. Gerard pulled himself together, using good sense not to prolong the situation any further: "You know what, let's go. I really don't need this."

Anthony saw what I saw and as they turned away to leave he made certain to let Gerard know where he stood in all of this. He is usually quiet but I don't know where this 'man' suddenly appeared from:

"Hey!" he shouted, getting Gerard's attention. "You had better not lay a hand on him." He moved in closer towards Andy in an effort to assure him that he would defend him. "Andy, you don't have to go."

"Anthony, it will be better if I do go. I, too, am not really welcomed here." Andy sounded like he was brainwashed.

"Oh, please, that's not true, Andy, and you know it," replied Anthony.

Anderson knew how much I loved him although I hated the choices he had made concerning his sexuality. I do not believe that anyone is born gay. God created us; there is no way He would make something that He detests. We are made in the image and likeness of God. When God created the animals, including man, he made them male and female. I tried to talk to Andy to persuade him not to go with Gerard but it was no use; he had his mind made up. I wondered whose mind it actually was.

I was crying and sobbing and wondering what in

91

the world would happen next. The limo was waiting since it was time to go home. I kept wondering how in God's name such a perfect day could end like this. My heart ached for my son. Just before I entered the vehicle, Sonja grabbed me by the arm; she was concerned, as always, being my darling friend.

"I have never seen this side of you, Melinda. What was that?"

"Why can't I want the very best for my sons?"

"Who says you can't, but you have to control yourself as well."

"That lifestyle is an abomination, Sonja."

"A lot of things are abominations; this is not your fault!"

"Oh yeah, well why do I feel like it is?"

I pulled myself loose from her grip and boarded the limo. The drive home began very quietly; no one said a word for quite some time. My head was full. I knew that I was wrong to behave that way and so I broke the silence by apologising for my behaviour, but I made it quite clear that my position on homosexuality was not going to change.

"Mom, all of us feel the same way about homosexuality," said André.

"I am very concerned about Andy; it looks like he is abused quite often. We will need to check on him tomorrow."

"When is he due to leave?" Sonja asked as she pulled out a piece of paper to write.

"He told me that he is leaving on Wednesday," said

Aphelia.

Sonja told us about a Dr. Matthews who had been dealing with people with homosexual tendencies for many years. He counseled with the Bible and his purpose was to ensure that his patients understood the devastating effects of homosexuality both spiritually and physically. I only hoped that this would work because I did not know what to do myself. Judging from my behaviour tonight, I would further destroy my son rather than help him.

Anton was deep in thought and was surprisingly very quiet. "Anton, what's up? I asked.

"Nothing really; just pondering on my life. Right now I feel like I am an abuser as well." Anton had begun to feel troubled about his promiscuous lifestyle. Although he persistently teased André because of his faith in the love that he shared with Aphelia, he turned to his brother with a befuddled yet appreciative look on his face.

"André, I couldn't take my eyes off you and Aphelia tonight. I still don't know how you did it. You believed with all your heart that she would come back and she did. You even had a dazzling rock waiting. Where did you get this extra positive attitude, man? I would see women and they would give me what I want, but after that I really don't bother much about them. I have not even thought of anything on a long term basis."

"Well, you have to do something about that, bro. Else you will never get anything like this." And he tenderly caressed Aphelia's cheek for a moment. André teased Anton but was actually very serious.

The limousine came to a stop. It was 12:30 a.m. and I was pooped. Everyone was exhausted and retired to bed almost immediately. I was the last one left. I too was tired but suddenly all my strength came back and I couldn't sleep.

I sat at the kitchen table with a cup of coffee replaying the entire day in my head. André came back downstairs for some water and was surprised to see me up.

"I thought you went to bed, Mom. What are you doing up still?"

"I can't sleep. I am worried about Anderson."

"Yeah, I am too but this is one of the things you place in God's hands."

"Come on, André, no more God talk."

"Mother!" When he addresses me like that I know I have touched a nerve.

"Are you blind? Can you not see the hand of God at work? How can I not attribute everything to Him? Come on, Mom, the Spirit of the Lord is beckoning, but you fight daily to get rid of Him. How are you going to stand? How are you going to live? Jesus said, 'I am the way, the truth and the life. No man comes to God but by me.' For as many as received Him to them gave He the power to become the sons of God. You cannot do it by yourself, Mom. Stop trying to be a super hero. You are human!"

André said those words almost in anger, speaking from his heart. But how can I do this? I have too many hang ups, too much hurt, too much pain, and I don't know how to give it over to God. Place them in God's hands. Where are His hands?

"I am not ready, André."

"Not ready for what?"

"I am not ready yet. I have to fix my life first. I can't let God into this mess."

"Mom, you need to accept Jesus as you are. He will fix you. But that's not it. You are ready for Jesus, but you're just not ready to forgive."

André left me in the kitchen and went to bed. His words stabbed me in the heart, but I refused to forgive. I intended never to forgive George, dead as he was. I will never forgive nor forget. I deserved the right to hold on to this for as long as I needed to. I will not forgive him for ruining my life. If things were different I would have had my family closer to me. Anthony is so withdrawn, Anton is way too promiscuous for his own good, André is fanatical about God and Anderson, oh God, Anderson. If only George had been different the boys would have stayed at home and I would have had a better handle on them. George is to be blamed for this entire situation. Forgive? I cannot forgive.

I finished my coffee then started upstairs. I tried to climb the stairs but suddenly I could not. I had this feeling in my stomach which moved to my head – I then saw an image like it was painted on the wall, only there was no wall in front of me. I yelled for André because I could not move. I slumped to the floor. He came running and he stooped beside me. "What happened, Mom?" he asked as the others came from their rooms as well.

"I am certain that I saw a vision," I started to explain. "It had to be a vision. I am not asleep and I am not dreaming. I was trying to walk up the stairs and I saw death. I saw a dead man; I saw Anderson dead." There was an indescribable pain in my heart at that time and tears streamed from my eyes. "There was so much blood and it seemed like his spirit was calling me. I could not talk to him; his head was hanging to the side. He was dead but yet he was calling me. I saw him but he couldn't see me."

I was not only crying by then but groaning in pain. André helped me to my room. He prayed with me and asked God to reveal the meaning of the vision to me. I really liked how Sonja and Aphelia backed up the prayer. The others remained silent. They laid their hands on my head and were saying, "Yes, Lord" and 'Amen' to phrases in the prayer as André prayed. Sonja did not speak in English all the time. "What was that?" I wondered; but I was too weak to even ask. My body gave up and I had to lie down. They went back to their rooms as I was beginning to fall asleep. As André was closing my bedroom door, in a whisper I said to him, "André, I think Andy is already dead."

"Mom, don't think about that now okay. Try to dream pleasant dreams."

He left and softly closed the door behind him. There were voices in the corridor but I could not understand what they were saying. I hoped they believed me because the vision was too real. I did try to put it out of my head though and fell asleep shortly afterwards. While they prayed, André asked God to grant me 'sweet sleep'. I guess his prayers were answered. The experience left me drained and I slept uninterrupted until the next morning.

Chapter Six

The smell of freshly brewed coffee engulfed me. It was morning, a new day. Sonja had brought me breakfast in bed. I felt the atmosphere was rather humid for morning time. I looked at my clock and realised it was really not morning but almost noon.

"Good day, Sleeping Beauty," said Sonja, with a cheery smile on her face.

"Why didn't you wake me sooner? The sun is hot."

"There was no need to do that. I don't think anyone got up early today. Well, except for André and Aphelia. They got up early and went to church."

"You didn't want to go with them?"

"Somebody had to stay here with you."

"I can take care of myself," I said trying to lift my body off the bed.

"Uh huh" replied Sonja and she helped me to get up.

"God, I feel lazy."

"That's because you finally let go of the tight grip you had on yourself."

"Maybe," I said stretching so long I could almost touch the ceiling.

I was starved. Sonja sat with me and I ate everything she had on the plate. I remembered the events of the night before but it just swiftly whisked across my mind. Sonja and I were still catching up and although I wanted to talk about my vision and her not speaking English while praying, I decided not to burden her too much at that moment. The vision really bugged me though because I knew that I did not imagine it. She started on a completely different topic and I stayed on course with her.

"You won't believe this, Mel, but André and Aphelia have decided to get married in four weeks."

"Oh, my God, can we plan a wedding that fast?"

"Well, we better. I have some vacation leave inside so I will call in and get it."

"Are you saying that I have you here for a month?"

"Yep, five weeks actually -- for the wedding and then for your birthday."

"Then you better get used to my bad behavior, Sonja."

"You have been bad all your life, Mel. It did not happen overnight," she said with a smile.

A wedding - my son was getting married - I couldn't be happier! I must remember that this is not my wedding but theirs. So I tried to counsel myself not to take over the planning but just to assist. However, I knew for certain that Sonja and I would have a ball of a time planning the wedding of our children. She was obviously ecstatic.

"Did you think this day would really come, Mel?"

"You know, I honestly didn't, but when you told me Aphelia was here and that she wanted to surprise André, I became hopeful. Only since he moved back here I realised that he still had deep feelings for her. André never gave up hope; he had been telling us that she was definitely coming back."

"Really? Aphelia told me about her feelings a couple months ago. It seemed like a new thing for her."

"Well, he knew for a while now, I tell you." I went to get the phone which was ringing.

"Hello," the voice on the other end was familiar.

"Harold?" I asked. "How did you get my number?"

I tried to get away from Sonja who was jumping up and down in excitement.

"Listen, I'm really sorry about…"

I did not finish, he cut me off saying that there was no need to apologise. My phone number was still the same and Harold still had it written down somewhere. He just wanted to know if I was alright and if I had slept well. I told him I did and we chatted for a little while with Sonja dancing in my face.

"Lunch? Well I am, I … you cooked?"

Sonja could only guess what the conversation was all about and she kept nodding her head up and down while she jumped up in front of me.

"Hold on a sec, Harold."

I blocked the mouth of the receiver and whispered to

Sonja: "He said the restaurant catered for a luncheon today and he would like to bring food for the entire family."

"He cooked on the first date? Charming."

"What first date? Anyway I am telling him no."

Sonja grabbed the phone from my hand and with the other hand held me at arm's length while she told Harold how wonderful his suggestion was and that we would be delighted. This is the one time I despised her gift. She could speak in almost any voice she wanted and often impersonated teachers at school. She was a riot. Harold was clueless that he was speaking to Sonja and not to me. She then hung up.

"He'll be here at 2:30. I guess I should put the chicken back into the freezer."

"Are you ever going to change?"

"I'm too old to change. Pull yourself together, get dressed and get downstairs."

"And if I decide not to come downstairs?"

"Mel, don't get me angry. You wouldn't like me when I'm angry."

"Fine! Let me call Anderson first, okay. I'll see you in a while."

"Great," she replied as she headed for the door and without turning around, she cautioned me, "and put on something sexy."

"I thought you got saved!" I yelled after her. She paused momentarily then flung her hair behind her and continued walking, laughing all the way down the stairs.

All attempts to reach Anderson proved futile and for a moment I assumed the worst. Nevertheless I had to convince myself that everything would be fine. The vision was etched into my mind though, in 3D. How do I get rid of that? At that point I could only hope that Anderson would call me back.

I took a shower then peered into my closet for something to wear. My God, Sonja really had me looking for something sexy; I could not believe myself. I did however find a yellow cotton dress that I had bought at West Mall the year before. I had never worn it and thought that this would be the perfect occasion. It was a cool house dress; the yellow was not blinding yet brighter than downy feathers, knee length, and an elasticized sleeveless top; an A-line styled skirt fell loosely from the hips. I liked the style because it hid my stomach a little. My hair was short and well, it is what it is, I cannot style it differently. I accessorized the dress with a tiger eyed jewel set that Sonja had brought for me.

When I was through I looked at myself in the mirror. Who was this woman looking at me? Did I know her? The clothing was familiar but behind this outer glamour there was an inner being that was hurting, grieving and crying out for help. The funny thing is that help had presented itself many times before but I had rejected it. I want to live but Christianity seemed so boring and straight jacketed; I didn't know if I could cope with that. I did however know that it was the only way out of my prison; but it took me into another prison. Did I want to be a prisoner of Christ?

Merry voices disturbed my thoughts and I realised that André and Aphelia were back and Anton had already commenced his heartless teasing. I got myself together and ventured downstairs to join the rest of the family. Sonja had them setting the table already; I noticed that there were eight place settings.

"Who's the eighth place for?"

"Just in case Anderson shows up," she replied hopefully.

"I didn't reach him, only the answering machine."

"Don't worry, Mel, he'll call."

Aphelia came in from the kitchen with André, the two of them giggling as if they had just met.

"Hi, Aunty Mel, did you have a good night?"

"I slept well darling. Was the guest room comfy enough for you?"

Anton had to be his usual self and put in his two pence, and of course it had to be about sex.

"There was a comfy room calling her last night but she played hard to get."

Aphelia hit him with the dish towel across his chest.

"Shut up, player!" she said, "I don't need to play hard to get. I made a choice."

"Boy, why does sex define you? Is that all you ever think about?" Anthony asked,

"What else is there to think about?" replied Anton

"What about the purpose for sex and the consequences or maybe the very attributes the one you're having sex with is looking for, like love, commitment, intimacy, huh?"

"And where in your life is all of this, Anthony?"

"I don't need to brag like you to prove that I am a man."

"The proof is in the pudding," replied Anton.

I was beginning to think that Anton was a coward and maybe he was just not telling the truth about his life. Maybe he was looking for love and could not find it. Maybe he scarred himself so much with his romantically insecure and irresponsible rampage that now the women ran from him. He was definitely showing signs of discontentment with his life, and obviously jealous of the relationship that André and Aphelia had. He continued to tease but his comments were getting out of hand and André thought it was time to pull the plug on him.

"André, after all that romantic dancing and dinner and the ring and all, didn't you feel like finishing the night with some real excitement?"

André was drying the water glasses with a napkin and stopped a while. He looked at Anton and replied.

"With a girl as enticingly sexy as Aphee, whom I love with every beat of my heart, of course I wanted to have sex. I am alive and I have emotions. I am human."

Anton did not expect that answer. He was really expecting him to say 'no'. His tilted head and wide opened eyes showed that he was puzzled but allowed André to continue.

"However, I think with my brains, Anton, and not with my sex organs. My body listens to me. When you put God in control of your life you can do anything. If you have some money that you want to save to utilize at a specific time, you put it on a fixed deposit. It matures when the time is right and then you will reap the benefits, not so?"

"Yes," replied Anton, "but where are you going with this?"

"Sex is like a fixed deposit. God deposited the desire for sex in us from birth. The time will come when it will mature and we will reap the full benefits from that deposit. If I break my fixed deposit before the appropriate time I will lose 'interest' both tangible and intangible. I don't want to be like you."

Anthony walked towards the kitchen. "Does anyone else need a cold drink?"

"No," I replied, "but you can bring a potato sack for Anton to cover his face."

We all laughed. Sonja and I were both amazed at the wisdom that André displayed. Since he committed his life to God he had become the epitome of wisdom. His older brother could not respond to that one and he remained quiet. Pointing his finger at Anton, André continued: "Starting from now, I would like you to stop with the sex talk. It is disrespectful to women; and as you can see, we have some fantastic women in this family: my intended, my mother and my future mother-in-law."

I was pleased that Anton heard this from a man and not a woman. It is sad how he disrespected women and someone had to tell him like it is. He had nothing to say now at all; he was just pondering on the wise counsel of his younger brother.

"You gotta stop, Anton," André continued shaking his head. "Unlock yourself from that prison; you're going too far."

The doorbell rang preventing Anton from responding to André. He was probably relieved, saved by the bell. He went to answer it and found that Harold had arrived with the lunch as promised. The guys went to assist in bringing in the containers from the car. He came in and placed his restaurant-style stainless steel serving trays on the table. He treated us with a very high standard of professionalism and we were pleasantly surprised. Sonja looked at me and I looked at her but said not a word. He was wearing a Navy blue suit with a predominantly white striped shirt and a tie. Why was he dressed like that I thought? So formal for a simple lunch at home! It was as though he was reading my mind.

"Excuse my attire, I came directly from church. I didn't have time to go home and change."

"Well, take off your jacket and tie and relax a little," I replied.

I took the clothing from his hands and placed them on the rack. He did say church, didn't he? God, are you setting me up? Everyone I love now goes to church. Oops, my thoughts slipped. Did I love Harold? Oh, my God! Get it together, girlfriend; be cool. We sat down to lunch and had a wonderful time. Harold brought so much food we had to put up the rest for another day.

At lunch André and Aphelia formally announced that they had chosen June 27th for the wedding; that was the week before my 50th birthday which was July 5th. We now had a wedding to plan, but like every other young woman, Aphelia had been planning her wedding in her head for a long time and knew what she was looking for.

"If I can contribute to your happiness, you guys can have the wedding at my place," Harold suggested.

"Aunt Mel, I will love to have it there. That place is the bomb."

"Okay, how many people can it hold?"

"One hundred seated comfortably and a little over with a push."

Aphelia thought that the capacity was sufficient for the family and close friends that she had planned to invite.

"Well, let's do the menu, Aphelia," Sonja added, "so that Harold can give us an estimate."

This was too good to be true and usually it is. I'll just have to wait and see. The boys did not care about planning a wedding. André rose and was too happy to leave the ladies alone with the hard work.

"My part is easy: Mom, you are the mother giver. Anthony you are my best man being the eldest of us all and Anton and Anderson are groomsmen. If you have more bridesmaids than that Aphee, I'll get a couple of guys from the Worship team, okay?"

"Okay," she replied with that little twinkle in her eyes, their secret code.

"Good, I'm done."

We all kind of got scattered at that point. I had asked the boys to go and find Andy, so they were about to embark on their journey. Sonja and Aphelia sat at the table working on a menu and other important things for the wedding, and Harold and I went into the kitchen to do the dishes. We worked silently for a while with only a little comment here and there. I could not help myself, thinking thoughts that were out of order. I felt guilty though since George has been dead for less than a week, buried three days ago and here I was, igniting feelings for another man. However, Harold was really no stranger to me at all; I did like him at one time and he had liked me.

Those were the days we sang duets at Anne's restaurant. We did not date officially but met every weekend at the restaurant and shared a table between performances. He knew I was married but I flirted with him, dangerously, and he responded. We kept a little distance though and although I knew how he felt, he never really stepped out of line but respected my marriage. He would touch me and hold hands on stage but we could have easily chucked that up to the performance; we knew differently though. I just had to ask him about his personal life a little. Why? Only God knows but I wanted to know what was going on with him.

"What became of Evelyn, Harold? I was so sure you two were going to get married."

"She did not want to marry; turned me down cold."

"Really? You have any kids."

"Nope."

"What did you do with your life?"

"Worked hard as hell!"

We laughed – I was kinda glad that he had neither wife nor kids but I also needed to know about the church thing and if there was a significant other.

"So you went to church today?"

"Yep, I've been going for a while now."

"What do you get out of going to church?"

"It's not what I get out of church. It's what I get out of serving the Lord."

Oh my word, another one! This must be your path, I teased myself. I knew the language they spoke, I could tell that Harold was 'born again' and not just going to a church building every week; he was the church.

"Are you seeing anyone now? I asked bravely, without thinking about it.

"No. The last time I went on a date was about eight months ago. Incidentally, her name was Mel, but that was short for Melissa and not Melinda."

"Life can be so interesting," I said.

"For sure, but I must admit that I really spent my time building the business. However, that date did not go too well, after that I decided that it was time to settle and to get serious, but I haven't met anyone to do that with yet."

Okay, so he was free, single and disengaged. What on earth did that mean? Harold reached across me to get the wash cloth from the edge of the sink. I jumped back, my actions clearly saying: 'Don't touch me!' He frightened me. I think I let the cat out of the bag. With sheer shock on his face, he raised his hands as if to say, "Okay, okay!" He looked me straight in the eyes, "What did that man do to you?"

"I'm sorry ... I didn't mean to..."

"It's okay." He said as he tried to make me feel comfortable again.

"How's the family handling George's death?" Harold

changed the subject, no doubt thinking that I really should be grieving.

"I think we are doing well because we've been expecting him to die a year now. So although it is difficult, I think it is less painful because we knew."

"I know that death is agonizing. We had a tough time when my father died, but God is a comforter"

'That's right," I said as we finished washing up his utensils.

Harold then packed up all his stuff. I thanked him for the lunch and for the kindness he had shown. As he was about to get into his car he handed me his call card, "Would it be alright if I called you again sometime?"

"Sure, why not. I will probably even visit "Le Paradis Magique" soon so we can sing again. I really enjoyed it actually."

"That will be great, Mel. Well, see you soon and take care. Bye!"

He drove off and I was really left wondering if there was anything to all of this at all. Only time would tell. I went back indoors and joined Sonja and Aphelia in planning the wedding.

The boys returned with no news - Andy seemed to have vanished. They found out he had checked out of his hotel room and when they went to his apartment, the landlord who lived downstairs said that Andy had left about two months ago. We were all unaware of that. Maybe if he had a land-line we would have known. I did not like it at all, remembering the vision I had seen the night before. I didn't know what it meant, but I did not like it one bit. My emotions got the better of me. I tried to control myself but I couldn't. I started to cry softly and my other sons gathered around me to provide comfort. I reminded them of the vision. They had first thought that Anderson just did not want to talk to us at this time but now they were beginning to get worried themselves. Anthony and Anton asked if I wanted them to stick around a little longer rather than go back to their homes and I definitely said yes to that. I wanted to call the police but Anthony reminded me that we had to wait forty-eight hours before we could report him missing. Everyone wanted to keep a positive mind but not me – it was not so much that I wanted to be negative; I was just scared because of the vision. I suggested that we should check his workplace; maybe he had not resigned yet to go away with Gerard. How was I supposed to survive the rest of the day? Suspense is truly a killer.

I left everyone downstairs and went to my room. I really had to talk to God a little bit. I wanted him to bring Anderson home to me. I did not want to lose my son – no way! I stretched out on the bed face down and I cried, and cried and cried. I could not help but think that I was responsible for his not having anything to do with me. Maybe I should have accepted him as he was and not try to change him. If only I was nicer to Gerard, he probably would have called us. I had a million unanswered questions and another million theories - maybe this or maybe that. My heart could not take anymore. I cried myself to sleep and when I woke up the next day I was in the same position on my bed. The only difference was that someone had pulled the covers over me and turned off the lights.

Chapter Seven

et another day, a day that the Lord has made; can I rejoice and be glad in it? I was still wearing my yellow dress as I never got undressed the night before. It was about 4:30 a.m.; I quickly undressed and put on my robe. I then went downstairs into the kitchen to get a cup of coffee. As usual, I just had to sit in my rocker and welcome in the morning. I began to ponder on my life and watch the sun burst through the sky while I sipped the soothing Nescafé blend that I loved so much.

I knew that that day was going to be a tough one. We had planned to call Anderson's workplace to see if they knew anything. Aphelia also needed to call a number of her girlfriends to ask them to be bridesmaids and all that went along with that. Then we wanted to start shopping for the wedding. I had to make an early move in order to get everything done. After a while, I got dressed but just before I ventured out, the boys had come knocking. Anthony had taken off his cell phone a couple days before and in turning it on again he saw a message from Andy. I was elated to hear the news but the elation did not last long at all.

The message read ...

> *"Anthony, I am fine. Please tell mammy that I will be okay.*
> *You all do not need to look for me. I am going away a little*
> *sooner than planned. I love you all, bye."*

They thought that this was an answer for me but I was not at all convinced that Andy had sent that message. The message was sent from his phone but it definitely was not from him. I started to tell them all the little things that did not add up.

"Firstly, Andy never calls me 'mammy' and then his text messages are always in short cut. You know, he would not spell out the word 'you'; he would just type the letter 'u'. This entire message was just too formal and grammatically correct. Andy did not send texts like that. Why would he do something that is so out of character all of a sudden? Sons, something is wrong. Something is wrong."

They listened to me although they thought I should let it go. We then called Andy's workplace and they informed us that Andy had resigned about three months ago. Things were getting stranger and stranger so we decided to go to the police right away instead. After interviewing all of us they simply said that it looked as though he had run away with his boyfriend and that there was no evidence of anything else. But I knew that something was wrong; nothing could be as accurate as a mother's instinct.

That vision remained in my head and I just knew that I was not mistaken but I eventually decided to keep all my feelings to myself. I prayed and hoped in secret but did what I did best: hide my true feelings. No one knew that I still kept looking for answers and was determined to find out what had happened to my son. If he was dead I wanted to bury him. If he had really decided to go away, I wanted to know that for sure. I needed closure.

We then went on to accomplish our agenda. We did a lot that day: the wedding notices went up, the invitations were ordered, and the colour scheme for the bridal party was chosen. While we were still out, Harold called Sonja to say that he was coming over to discuss the menu. Sonja knew full well that that could be done on the phone but she wanted him to come. She just had to push, would not let it go. We got home later in the day and were really wiped out. However we were anxious to see what Harold had put together with Aphelia's ideas for the menu and so waited for him to arrive.

All of us sat on the porch around the fountain. Its water has always produced a calming effect. We had eaten lunch pretty late while we were on the road and no one was really interested in dinner. Rufus was still missing. He never did not come back; evidently, he was gone for good. The boys all had to return to work the next day, having used up their three days bereavement leave. Anthony thought it a good idea to drive with André but André harshly protested.

"No way, man!, You never leave at four o'clock."

"Well, I am not feeling like work these days actually, so I will leave early."

"Anthony, I am saying this in front of many witnesses: I will leave you in San Fernando if you are not by my car at 4:10 p.m."

André had good reason to come home immediately after work; after all, Aphelia was here. He was not letting up on his bigger brother at all. I butted in because I had a different agenda: "Why don't you guys just put in for leave and stick around here a little longer, until the wedding at least."

I had it in my heart to ask that for a while but I was unsure of how they would interpret it. It was a tall order; they had not stayed here at all for as long as I could remember and now I was asking them to stay for six weeks. I was pleasantly surprised at the response. Anthony reminded André of the new policy that was issued at the company that encouraged all those with vacation leave stacked up to take some of it or get paid for the leave instead.

"I'll pull some strings, André, to get it approved without us even going down there."

"You think H.R. will grant it without filling out the forms?"

"Family emergency! Yes they will. Who is the boss, boy?"

Laughter erupted on the porch. Just imagine Anthony made a joke – he barely even speaks. We were concentrating so intensely on our own issues that we completely forgot he was in a position at the company to make certain decisions. He is so humble concerning his accomplishments, you won't hear him boasting and he is not haughty.

"What about you, Anton?" I asked hoping for a similar response.

"I can take some leave I suppose and the semester just ended so I have no evening classes until September."

"It's settled then. I can't tell you how much this means to me."

At this point I still had no clue as to what action I would pursue to find Anderson. I only wanted to keep an eye on the others for a while longer. Their presence strengthened me, I needed that. All I had for years were phone calls and short visits or we just met for lunch once in a while. I thank George for dying; it gave me my life back. I have asked myself time and time again if I was being selfish; and I have also answered myself time and time again, 'No you're not'. That beast took my dignity, my life, my hopes and my dreams but I pretended just so that my kids would learn how to handle covenant relationships as the wedding vows state: for better or for worse; in sickness and in health, 'till death do us part. I am free now – death having parted us.

It began to drizzle slightly just as Harold parked his vehicle and trotted up the walkway.

"Nighty night, everyone."

He greeted us then sat in the only empty chair on the veranda, directly opposite my chair. He immediately began to unfold his plan for the wedding meal. I don't think I heard a word that he said because my mind was racing. I remembered that Harold used to work at a private investigating firm. He gave it up for the management position at Anne's. This could be the opportunity that I needed to get this thing done. I had to devise a plan to secretly look for Anderson. Harold was accustomed to hearing people's problems and investigating their situations so maybe he would do the same for me or at least he might know someone who could. Could I trust him with my story? I was so desperate I was willing to try. In any case you won't know 'till you try.

Sonja and Aphelia were simply loving the ideas and

agreeing to everything. He had made it so simple for them. He gave them the costing, and then sat with us a little while longer.

Sonja excused herself and went indoors; Aphelia followed shortly afterwards. The boys then decided to shoot hoops in the backyard and so Harold and I were left alone on the porch. I was not sure how much I should say but I thought I would just begin to speak and let it flow. At that point I was willing to do anything to find my son.

I started by apologising for being so edgy in the kitchen the day before. Harold had a couple of questions concerning that episode and decided to ask them. I used that opportunity to share the problems with George and the alienation of my sons. I had no idea how after all these years I finally mustered the strength to talk to someone other than Sonja, but I wanted Harold to help me so I decided to be completely honest with him. For some strange reason I trusted him; but I also thought that if he knew everything and had any kind of interest he would step back if he could not handle it and I would avoid being hurt again. Seeing him again did bring back memories of the platonic love affair we had.

Harold listened attentively for approximately an hour and I held nothing back. I made certain to tell him that apart from Sonja, he was the only person who was privy to that information. There was a look in his eyes that resembled sadness and grief. I thought I might have said too much.

"I did not mean to burden you at all. Maybe this was a mistake."

"This is no mistake. I am glad that you are telling me all this. It's okay – you need to throw off the burdens sometimes."

I was happy that the tense emotions between Harold and me back then never went beyond holding hands. I knew I had sent mixed messages because I did like him but was committed to my marriage regardless of the state it was in. I would leave the restaurant and think about Harold for days on end, but did not have the strength or the courage to act on my feelings. It would not have been fair to him anyway, dating a married woman and I suppose he too restrained himself from doing that.

"I admire your strength. I pray that God will heal the hurt. But I must say, Melinda, in order for you to move on, you must forgive him."

I could not believe that he said that. I shook my head but really had no intentions of forgiving George. Now was the time for me to ask Harold the big question.

"Will you help me find Andy?"

"Of course, Melinda. Anything you need just let me know."

I responded immediately to those encouraging words.

"I need a private investigator."

Harold agreed that a private investigator was a safe way to begin. He decided to start the preliminaries himself and if he saw something that was worth checking out further he would suggest I hire a crew. The first thing I thought he should check was the airlines to see if Anderson had left the country at all. He agreed and promised to begin the very next day. Harold left that night giving me a final word of assurance. As he was walking down the stairs he suddenly stopped, turned and came back up looking directly into my eyes.

"Melinda, I want you to know that I have always liked you. In fact, I think I have loved you for as long as I can remember. As a man, I apologise, on behalf of George, for the horrors that you have endured over the years. With God on my side, I will make certain that you find your son and I will also make certain that you never ever feel any such pain again, as long as you would allow me."

He reached out and took my right hand, lifted it up to his face and kissed it, not looking for me to respond to his heartfelt speech. He then turned and walked slowly out of the yard, into his car, popped the horn then drove off. My jaw dropped so low it could touch the ground. What breed of man is this? I wondered as the car disappeared around the corner. George never apologised for anything. Is there a man out there that would really make me feel safe in his presence? I just had to set my mind on things that seemed to make sense. I could not think of Harold any other way than the man I hired to find my son. I was overjoyed that he was willing to assist me. That was my focus. I knew that I would be seeing a lot of him and that I should just let things be – time will tell. I then locked up the house and went upstairs hoping to go straight to bed, but Sonja was waiting for me.

She wanted to know what on earth we talked about for so long. I was not willing to spill the beans. I knew that she would confide in Aphelia, then Aphelia would confide in André, then my secret would no longer be a secret. I thought quickly about how I would answer and I told her that we were just catching up. I did tell her how he kissed my hand and she was carrying on like a mad lady. I did it purposely to throw her off about the real reason I had had the conversation with Harold.

We heard the piano downstairs. André probably

could not sleep either. It was the first time since they arrived that André was playing at night. Sonja thought it was lovely. I told her that his music and singing were so tranquillizing; it could soothe a tired soul and somehow you could go to bed with God on your mind and wake up with His praises on your lips. I honestly believe that it was his music that had kept me going while I took care of George. I would be so tired at night, completely worn out by George's insults and the demands that the paralysis placed on me. I don't know why I did not put him in a nursing home; too late now to even waste time thinking about that.

I went to bed that night with a feeling of relief, at least there was one person who believed me when I said that something was really wrong where Andy was concerned.

The week passed quickly. The house became a buzz of activity. Aphelia hosted her bridesmaids for fitting and accessorizing. The boys spent a lot of time together. Everyone thought that I was dating Harold. I just let them think whatever they wanted. My focus was on finding Andy and I refused to lose sight of it.

It was a Friday night, the perfect night for a date. Harold and I had already faked a couple lunch dates this week so that we could meet to discuss Andy's case and we had another that night because he had some information for me. He picked me up around seven. I was strangely being drawn to him once again; I noticed things that I had not noticed before: he had the cutest dimples, an extremely agreeable disposition and a smile that revealed perfectly set white teeth; they can't be real, I thought – not at his age. Either I was falling in love or simply loved the fact that he was assisting me.

I took pleasure in the way he dealt with the

situation and how he treated me with honour. He opened car doors, pulled out my chair, ordered on my behalf, walked me into the house, and had only good things to say about my choice in clothing – everything that a woman would like a man, who claims he loves her, to do. Best of all, he never disrespected me in the slightest form. I wanted to make certain that I knew exactly what was happening between us. I did not want to mix up the emotions with regards to the situation. It seemed Harold sincerely cared about finding Anderson. Each day he got more and more into it so I felt his response was just one of pure concern for Andy and did not have anything to do with me. He remained focused. Although he made me feel special, he placed all the emphasis on Andy. I kept my feelings to myself and made certain not to do anything to blur the purpose.

The first major news came in. A check with all the airlines proved that Anderson never left Trinidad – at least not using his real name or his passport. That was a great start but there was a lot more to do in order to get the police involved. I also had some information of my own to share, Anthony had received another text message supposedly from Andy. The information rendered it even stranger than the first.

It read ... *"Anthony I am doing fine here in Canada. How is mummy doing? Say hello to all for me, bye."*

We already knew that Andy could not be in Canada. Harold thought that he should start looking into this Gerard guy. We knew neither his last name nor where he worked. Harold decided to check the hotel to get credit card records and his last name. We agreed that was to be the next step; he would then call me for us to plan another 'fake date' as soon as he got any information. Harold took me home and as usual he walked me to the door; we said our goodbyes, then he left.

The wedding plans were progressing and my plans continued full speed ahead as well. Harold and I did not meet during that week because the credit card information was not as forthcoming as he had expected. I told him that on the Friday coming he should come over for lunch and hang out just so we could keep up the farce.

We sat down to lunch that Friday. André thought it was time to let me know that he had to choose another groomsman for the wedding party. They had sent text messages to Andy about the wedding but had received no reply. He wanted to discuss the matter with me before calling the other guy to try on the suit. I agreed. It was still my position though that Andy was not in Canada and that someone else had sent the text but then I wondered why didn't the person keep up with the charade and reply to the text concerning the wedding. So maybe Andy did in fact send the text himself but wanted to stay far away from us. The vision flashed across my mind again. Why was I being reminded constantly of this – it was a gruesome picture. I could see Andy up against a wall, his hands and feet are bound, and there are cuts and bruises all over his body; there was a blood splatter on the wall behind him. This was really getting to me.

I decided however to focus completely on André's wedding. There was a very festive mood at our house and I did not want to spoil it. Everyone was jolly and André and Aphelia looked even more certain of this move than they ever were. George's study and the adjoining room on the left were converted into a small apartment for the new couple. The boys worked tirelessly at it. Aphelia's belongings arrived from New York and she spent hours unpacking and getting her home ready. The kitchen was next to the study and so they decided to share my kitchen and not add another. It was perfect – cute and cozy. André had not gotten rid of any of the stuff that Aphelia had left behind. She felt even more secure as she thought he must have had faith that they would be together again and so he had kept everything. She sorted through the boxes, threw away a number of things but kept those of sentimental value.

After lunch, Harold and I went onto the porch. We had been sitting there for about twenty minutes when a young man came to the house. He rang the bell at the gate and we beckoned to him to come up to the porch. He was dressed in a green shirt with black pants and a tie. In his hand were brown envelopes and we thought that he had come to deliver a package.

"Good afternoon. I am looking for Melinda Graham."

"I'm Melinda," I responded.

"My name is Keith. I work at Campton's Accountancy Firm."

"Oh, okay. Andy worked there," I replied. "What can I do for you?"

"I was wondering if we could talk – in private. It's about Anderson."

I looked at Harold and began to wonder what on earth was going on. However, I did not want a private conversation; he had to speak to Harold as well. I invited him in, and told him that Harold was a family friend so he could speak to both of us. We took him into the living room. I offered him a drink but he refused. He sat on the sofa and suddenly became very nervous.

"This is hard but I will just get to the point. I think

Anderson is in trouble."

"What!" I exclaimed.

"I know your son very well, Mrs. Graham. When you called last Monday, I took the call. The fact that you did not even know he left the firm worried me. Although I want to keep my life – our life, a secret, I have to come forward just in case my suspicions are correct. I believe that Anderson is a victim of a man named Gerard Maxwell."

"What in the world are you talking about, young man?"

As he began to tell the story, I stopped him; I thought that his brothers should hear it as well, and so I called everyone to the living room. I was even more convinced that I was on the right track all along. When they were all there, I briefed them and they sat down to hear what Keith had to say.

"I was gay. Anderson and I dated for a short while but before that, I dated Gerard. He is older than we are and very controlling. I did not allow him to control me though; so not long after we started the relationship he became abusive towards me. I resisted and fought back a lot. We broke up and made up like any other heterosexual relationship that is abusive."

The boys were in shock and visibly upset. I could see the pain as my eyes searched their faces around the room. Everyone kept silent so that Keith could tell the story. Something was going on in their heads. They were now totally in sync with me and my instincts.

"When I decided that I was getting out for good, everything went haywire," Keith continued as he made himself a little more comfortable. "When he thought he would lose me for sure, he took me to a remote place in

Cedros, pretended that he was sorry for everything and tried to make up for it by giving me a two-day holiday in the country. He has a house, or really a shack I should say, down there. It was a virtual prison and I immediately saw that he was up to something. There were gadgets on the walls with chains attached to them – I was scared like hell."

My head hurt, my heart ached, and tears streamed from my eyes. There were so many thoughts going through my mind at the same time, I could hardly keep up. Harold held my hand in an effort to comfort me. Keith continued his story.

"To cut a very long story short, I escaped from the house and I ran to the nearest village. I think it was almost a day before I saw another house or a person. I finally met a couple who took me to the hospital. I lied about the entire ordeal because I was ashamed. They just thought I was on drugs."

I was curious as to what happened to him and Gerard after that and so asked him straight out: "Did you see Gerard after that?"

"No, but I spoke to him. He called and threatened me about five times after that. I did not want to get the police involved at all and so I hired a gang banger to beat him up. After he got that beating I called him and told him not to call me ever again and if he did I will call the police. He left me alone since then. I never saw him again."

I had to ask some pertinent questions about Anderson to get to the bottom of it all. But I was amazed that Keith had come forward, since he really did not have to. This is probably the information we needed; but before he continued I told my family the truth about Harold and me - that we were not dating and that he worked for me as a private investigator. I informed them that we already knew that Andy did not leave the country and was in the process of finding out who this Gerard was. I had a few more questions for Keith and kept my composure. I really don't know how I managed that one.

"Tell me about your relationship with Anderson and what you think caused him to go with Gerard."

"I tried the gay thing but I know it is wrong. About six months into our relationship I was invited to a seminar that taught us how not to be gay. I really wanted out of that lifestyle and so I tried to follow the steps and was successful. Anderson, however, had refused to go to the seminar so I stopped seeing him even before the counseling. I got out of homosexuality and have been straight since. I never saw him with Gerard but I saw a picture of them. I did not tell Andy of my ordeal at all. One day, however, I took the picture from his desk and asked him about Gerard. We did not have a good relationship as he was still bitter about the breakup and told me to just stay out of his business, and I did."

"You never told him that Gerard was dangerous?"

"No.'

"Why? That could have saved him."

Harold held my hand tighter and told me not to put any blame on Keith but just to listen and we would come up with a plan.

"Mrs. Graham, I noticed that Andy had changed drastically over the past year. He was absent from work frequently and was very withdrawn. I copied the many warning letters and memos he got from work and I cleared out some things from his drawers that he had left behind."

"Why didn't he clean out his drawers after he resigned?' I asked.

"Because he just left work one afternoon and never returned; he did not officially resign. We got a phone call two weeks later."

"This is not like Andy at all. What do we do Harold?"

We sat and discussed the matter for a while and decided that we would go to the house in Cedros and check things out. Harold had to make a number of calls for advice and to come up with a plan. We thanked Keith and asked him if he would go with us to Cedros to show us the place. He agreed but was not sure if he knew exactly how to get there. Harold assured him that his people would know. He was hungry by then and so Aphelia and Sonja took him into the kitchen to get something to eat.

By six o'clock that evening, Harold had gotten three all-terrain vehicles and four policemen to go with us to Cedros. When they were ready to go, I also presented myself, eager to make the trip. They were not going to leave me here at all! I put on jeans, sneakers and a loose-fitting T-shirt. I had a bag packed with clothing for Anderson and a change of clothing for me. I packed towels and a first aid kit. I then went into one of the vehicles and sat down. They said everything they could to convince me to stay at home but there was no way that I could do that; the suspense would kill me. It was no use arguing with me at all, I did not budge. I was already in the vehicle and so they had no choice but to allow me to go with them. Sonja and Aphelia stayed at the house promising to pray us through. I hoped that she prayed in 'Tongues' again because she told me that only God could understand that Language - it was like speaking mysteries.

André sat next to me and for the entire three and a half hour drive, we said almost nothing. Keith was in the lead vehicle with Harold; Anthony and Anton were in the other one. André started praying softly, his eyes closed – he was on another planet. I peered through the window, my mind not clear on anything. It was already dark so there was not much to see. I looked to the heavens; the starry sky reminded me of a multitude of angels. I hoped that God would send His angels to help us. Tears began to flow from my eyes – André reached out and took my hands.

"Mom, God is with us. Everything will be fine." His words were reassuring; I cried even more. My cell phone rang – it was Harold.

"Melinda, how are you back there?" I gave André the phone; I could not speak because I was becoming overwhelmed by my emotions. André spoke to him and hung up. He left me alone to cry and to talk to God in my own way.

We finally got to Cedros. Thankfully, Keith remembered a lot more than he thought he would have and we found the house quite easily. It was up on a small hill that gradually ascended about twenty feet above the level where we had to park the vehicles. Small steps made out of the earth itself and chucked with steel prongs and wood made it easier for us to climb the hill. This was the only house in this area; the other house we saw was at least a mile down the road. I almost died when I saw Anderson's old car at the bottom of the hill. He said he had sold it but maybe he had sold it to Gerard. The pain caused by the anxiety coursed through every bone and muscle group of my body and my thoughts were racing. Is he here? Is he alive?

We parked the vehicles a little way off. The experts briefed us and we then slowly climbed the hill up to the property on which the house stood, surrounded by at least twenty to thirty feet of land on each side. The outside was well-kept; the grass was cut low. There were a few goats resting on the grass at one side. There were no dogs. I saw only a black and white cat. It seemed like all the lights in the house were on and there was movement inside. Suddenly, out of nowhere we heard someone shouting and stamping.

"Eat fool, eat; or else you will die! How on earth could I ever think that you were any good? Open your mouth! Open your mouth!"

The police signaled us to be quiet and they surrounded the house. They peeked in the windows, then called Keith and Anthony. André and Anton stayed very close to me. Keith and Anthony came back to the spot where I was standing; Anthony's eyes were filled with tears.

"Mom, he's in there. He's alive."

I started to run immediately but my boys held me back firmly and Anthony reassured me that the men knew what they are doing.

"They need to make sure the place is safe first, Mom. Hold on a little while longer; it will be over soon." Harold and one of the policemen then walked to the front of the house while the other three stood guard – one at the back and the others at the sides. They called out to the occupants of the house.

"Gerard! Police! Open up." There was no answer but definitely movement in the house. They called again.

"Gerard, open up. If you do not comply we will break

down the door."

We saw someone peeping through the window; he saw us and because of what we heard next I think he recognized that we were Andy's family. The curtains closed. There was a loud cry and something that sounded like a beating with a piece of wood: 'Whoop! Whoop! Whoop!' The men broke down the door and entered immediately with loud shouts. We all ran up to the house as well. As I ran I called his name loudly, "Andy!" Crying and shouting all at once. I entered the front door and then I came to an abrupt stop. The world spins on its axis so fast that we never feel it, but now I was so still that I felt the earth spinning. I saw my vision again – no, it was not a vision – this was the real thing. I stared in awe and horror at this dreadfully disgusting site: my son, tied up against a wall. There was blood all over him and his head hung to one side. He looked like death but, thank God, he was still breathing. You would think that my vision was a snap shot of this scene. Every cell in my body froze and began to hurt; but I revived quickly and ran towards him. I gently pulled on his tattered, blood stained clothing. Harold got the keys, unlocked the chains and took him down. He was very weak but he knew we were there.

"Mom," he barely whispered.

"Don't speak now, baby," I said as I held him close and tried to find out how badly hurt he was.

His brothers were in tears and stood in disbelief but everyone stood back and allowed me to be with Andy. The abuse was horrible, unimaginably ghastly, too much for any of us to bear.

Gerard was hand-cuffed and lay on the floor. The officers in the interim were looking around the house. One of them picked him up and started to walk him outside when he made a comment that angered my sons, "You are lucky; he was supposed to die tonight." Gerard probably thought that all Andy's brothers were feeble; he had no idea who he was talking to. I thought to myself, provocation is against the law; and I knew what was coming when I saw three pairs of eyes connect to each other. I shook my head, mouthing the word 'No!' I tried to stop them but it was no use. This was probably the first time that they used their Karate skills outside of the dojo. Both André and Anton were black belts in high school while Anthony achieved blue belt level and Anderson red belt. They did not follow through with the Martial Arts and discontinued training after leaving school but that night I saw the training in action and regretted for a moment signing them up for Karate classes. They communicated without words to beat this man silly.

Before Gerard could take the smirk off his face, they grabbed him from the hands of the officer and dealt him a few blows. I shouted for them to stop because I did not want them to get into trouble as Gerard was wearing handcuffs - he was defenseless. The policemen stood aside and did nothing for a little while then stopped them. The officer in charged looked at Anthony and said, "He resisted arrest." I knew that meant that they would take the responsibility for Gerard's beating. He was bleeding from his nose and mouth and as they took him away I noticed he walked with a limp. My sons did not reply but returned to help me with Andy who was still semi-conscious. Keith had stayed next to me but Andy did not recognize him.

The Cedros police were called and they took over the case. They searched the house and gave the okay for Andy to be taken to a hospital. I immediately inquired if he could be taken to a private hospital because of the sensitivity of the issue. I also did not want to travel this distance daily at all. They were concerned about traveling so far in his condition but agreed, though a little apprehensive. The Ambulance took us directly to a facility in Port-of-Spain. I rode in the ambulance and the boys followed behind with Harold. Keith remained with us throughout the entire ordeal. I was so exceedingly grateful to him for coming forward. Without his help Andy would have been dead. I talked to Andy for the entire trip, making certain that he did not fall asleep. The E.M.T. attendant was there but she allowed me the chance to be with him. She checked his vital signs from time to time.

We arrived at the hospital about 6:30 a.m. Andy was given immediate attention and was checked out thoroughly. He had two broken ribs, bruises and cuts from the beating, and there was evidence of sexual assault. Andy was okay otherwise, physically. I believe that most of the problems would be emotional and would show up afterwards. He had also been drugged by Gerard. He had to be detoxified so he really could not converse much at that time. I wanted to stay at his side and not move but the boys would not hear of it. They convinced me that I needed to go home, shower and sleep. I felt relieved and free although he was in such a state. I knew that Andy was safe at the hospital so I agreed to go home and rest.

Keith lived twenty minutes away in a small village called Carenage. We took him home first. I got his telephone number and promised to call him. I thanked him again and told him that I would never forget what he did for us. I wondered if I would have despised him as well if he was still gay. It is not as if I don't like gay people; I just can't understand their position on sexuality and believe that they are going against God's plan for humanity. However, I had no harsh feelings against Keith at all. Was it because he helped us – or was it because he had changed his life? I really did not know, but I did not spurn him at all.

On our arrival home, Sonja had coffee and other goodies ready and waiting but I could not eat. I needed to sleep. I asked Harold if he would stay on and he said he would. I reached out and hugged him. He responded by completely engulfing me in his arms. I said nothing – neither did he. We had a connection that could not be expressed with words. Our finite understanding would have made a mess of things if we dared talk.

I then left everyone downstairs and went up to my room. I did not plan not to return but the events that followed were completely out of my control. I turned on the shower, stood below it in all my clothing and cried non-stop for about half an hour. I wanted to talk to God but could not say a word. I could only cry. I thought only of God because I knew that it was He who had given us the sweet victory that day.

My vision was now like an abstract painting in my mind and not as real and in 3D as I had seen it before. It felt like a mission was over – a weight dropped from my heart. I had accomplished something. I stayed in the shower with my eyes shut. I was drenched with the water but I did not feel wet; I did not even feel tired anymore having been out all night. An unexplainable feeling took over my bathroom and it had me captivated. There had to be a God out there, not just an artist's impression of what Jesus, the Saviour, looked like – but a Being – a live Spirit. I screamed out to God.

"If You are real reveal Yourself to me, right here, right now." I meant it. Be careful what you pray for ... suddenly an awesome presence surrounded me. I felt as if someone's arms wrapped around me, hugging me tightly but so softly. I was alone in my room. No one was there with me. Still I felt those arms. "Jesus!" I cried, sniveling from deep within my being, "Heavenly Father, Gracious God!"

I cried out various names and attributes of God as a bright light exploded through the shower doors. The arms around me held me tighter. I knew that God Himself showed up. I gave in to the awesome presence that I felt. I started to worship God as the tears flowed like rivers from my eyes, taking my pain and washing it down the drain.

"Oh, God! I praise You. You are truly an awesome God. You are marvelous. You have showed up and given my family hope again. I surrender! I will serve You, Jesus. Whatever You need me to do I will do – just name it, God. How can I repay You for Your kindness towards me? How can I say thanks? I am nothing, inadequate. You are everything. Take my life and make me into what You want me to be .Oh, God! Oh, God!" I began to groan as words failed me. I did not know what else to say. I basked in the presence of the Lord. This was all for me ... God did this all for me ... nothing is as satisfying as this Holy atmosphere. I felt as I worshipped God He began to clean me thoroughly, right down to the cellular level. That was a great feeling and though I did not fully comprehend it, I knew that this was my moment and I could not break loose from it. I had asked for it – I had wanted a supernatural experience. God granted me my wish and if I had any doubts, they had all vanished. I had experienced Jesus for myself and there was no doubt in my mind anymore. Blessed be the Name of the Lord!

The light sort of dissolved after a while but I stayed there for maybe an hour or so just praying, calling each member of my family by name and laying out their personal situation to God. I prayed to God for forgiveness. I accepted Jesus that day, purposing to serve Him thereafter. How could I not serve Him; how could I turn my back? Could I pretend that the shower experience was not real? My denial would be like Moses denying the burning bush or Jonah the whale experience. I didn't know if I would ever get another chance to experience an awe-inspiring moment like that and so I did not want it to end.

All I knew was that the members of my family needed to experience this; Anthony needed the Lord and so did Anton. Anderson had lived through sheer hell and I had to show him that there was a way out.

So now I had become a Christian, what was next? How do I tell others that Jesus is real? I knew, however, that I could lean on the members of my family who had already experienced Jesus and so I would.

A song came to my mind: 'I got a joy, joy, joy, joy, down in my heart'. This joy was truly down in my heart. Another line says: 'I got the peace that passes understanding'. How many times have we sung that and were clueless as to what it means. For the first time I was at peace yet I had so much turmoil going on simultaneously. It was a peace that passed all understanding. I was not going to try to comprehend it but just remind myself that God is real. Jesus is Love – Jesus is Peace!

Chapter Eight

I was again awakened to the smell of freshly brewed coffee. Sonja came into my room with it. I felt blessed to have her with me during that time. She walked to the bed not certain if I was asleep or not. I turned around, looking at her with a broad smile.

"You're awake, Mel," she said and placed the coffee on my night stand.

"What time is it? What day is it?"

"Hmmm, you are free in spirit. It's 8:30 a.m. and it's Sunday. How are you doing?"

"I am absolutely rested and I feel fine, thanks."

I got up from the bed and thought I'd lost fifteen pounds. I was light in spirit but felt it in my body too. I sat down again and took the coffee. Yesterday's events then flashed across my mind.

"Andy! Did anyone go to see Andy?" I said that thinking that I had left him all alone.

"Yes, honey; don't fret! Aphelia and I went yesterday afternoon. We let everyone else rest."

"How is he?"

"Doing very well. I called again this morning. He is awake."

"Thank you, Sonja. I can't wait to see him."

"The doctor said that we could visit around 11:00. That's why I came to wake you up."

"Sonja, you won't believe what I've been through."

"André told us. God is great and greatly to be praised."

"AAAAmen," I replied, causing Sonja to look at me in a way that said, 'I feel you sister'. I think I sounded different – like a Christian. She immediately recognised the difference in language but she however, reserved her comments.

"Where is Harold?"

"He's downstairs as well. He came about fifteen minutes ago. Everyone is waiting for you at the breakfast table. Put your robe on and let's go down. You'll come back up to get dressed."

I did as she asked. I suppose they wanted to see if I was alive and I'm sure we had a few things to discuss. I was sprightly as I walked down the stairs. They looked at me as though they had expected me to wobble down the stairs but what they had not known yet was that I had met with Jesus during the night. I joined them at the table and the first item on the agenda was an apology for not listening to me and for not believing the vision. I did not act like 'I told you so'; something I would normally do. There was no need for that.

They also thanked Harold for being there for me. He just looked at me and smiled. That was no ordinary smile - I smiled back. Something had happened between us and I could hardly wait to see him privately. Aphelia and André were thinking of postponing the wedding so that I can concentrate on Andy's recovery but I would not hear of it. Generally I believe people must realise that choices have consequences and though I felt deeply for Andy, I knew that he still had to feel for himself and pull his own life together. There was no need to put off the wedding, no need for André to wait any longer. Andy was alive and he would be fine.

We visited Andy at the hospital. He was already doing a lot better. He was awake and alert and had eaten breakfast well that morning. The police also visited him to ask some questions. The doctor assured us that if he continued to progress at that rate he could go home the next day. I was overjoyed, I had taken care of Daddy and George and I was certain that I could take care of Andy as well. I hugged him and kissed him and apologised for everything. He was very receptive, relieved to be alive.

Andy told us that he had given up and thought that he would die. The last thing he remembered was waking up in the house, bound and gagged, with Gerard beating him with a belt as though he were a child. At first he thought it was a sick joke but quickly realised that he was in trouble. Anderson was quick to point out that my attitude towards Gerard had nothing to do with the kidnapping. He believed that this was planned a long time ago hence he was forced to leave the job and give up the apartment. We let him talk but the details were very difficult to listen to. He asked if we could take him home. We told him the doctor had already given us the ok to do so the following day. We talked a little longer and I promised to chain him to my hands so he could not step too far away from me again. He laughed heartily and I was glad to see that he could laugh.

We left the hospital around 2:30 p.m. On our way home we picked up pizzas. For the first time in years I did not have an issue on my mind. My head was now free, clear to see other important things and people – like Harold. I knew that I was falling in love with him. That episode of falling in love again felt like gravity was pulling me down from the clouds at high speeds. I was convinced, too, that the feeling was mutual. We still did not have the opportunity to be alone yet, something I wanted so badly because I was expecting a homily. How could I not love him, especially after all this? He stepped lightly on this issue and was extremely sensitive to my feelings but I think he would be uninhibited now. I made up my mind that I would not push him away but release myself to love again. I believed that I was deserving of someone to love, having been robbed of so much of my life. I had been alone for so long but had coped. Now these two weeks were just amazing; although they were filled with turmoil, they reminded me of what love is all about.

Sonja rode with us to the house. When we got there she got out of the car but Harold asked me to stay. He told Sonja that he was taking me into town for a short while and we would be back soon, as if I were a child needing Sonja's permission. My heart was pounding in anticipation of Harold's plans. He drove me to the lookout on Lady Young Road in Morvant. As we ascended the hill, taking in the scenic beauty of the Port-of-Spain skyline, Harold reached over and took my hand, gently squeezing it in the process. I turned to look at him but he looked straight ahead as he drove and did not turn to me. I felt safe – I liked the feeling.

This place is even more beautiful at night but with the increase of criminal activities on the island, the lookout is not as popular as it used to be. Harold walked over to the passenger side of the car and opened the door for me. He held my hands as I climbed out and led me almost to the edge of the precipice and we leaned against the barriers.

"Mel," he said holding both my hands and staring into my eyes, "isn't God marvelous? What a weekend!"

"The hand of God was surely with us over the past few days," I replied, shaking my head and remembering the events.

"Harold, I don't know where to begin to thank you for all your help. If ever there was someone 'God-sent', it is you."

Harold pulled me closer to him yet maintaining a respectful distance.

"You are an exceptionally beautiful woman. You have the heart of a servant and you are definitely the world's greatest mother. I have fallen completely and hysterically in love with you, but ..."

"But what?" I asked, enjoying every moment of that extraordinary occasion.

"Now that you have found Andy, you no longer need me."

"That may not necessarily be accurate, Harold."

"I am not ready to say goodbye," his stare saying a lot more than his words.

"Me neither."

"I want to explore the possibility of a relationship, you and me. I would like to see you now, for real."

"I've seen you in a different light these past weeks and I

hoped that you felt the same way that I did. I think I'm in love with you, too. I would be honoured if you continued to see me."

"That's it. So easy?"

"So easy," I replied with a smile that spoke a million words.

"I guess I don't need the speech I practiced then."

He stepped closer to me, lifted my hands up to his face and kissed them. He then hugged me gently. I savoured the moment but was somehow disappointed that he did not kiss me. I should have known that though, because a kiss can take you down a vicious path; not to mention a path that I certainly was not ready for just yet. A million thoughts went through my mind as Harold continued to hug me. He told me that he had been waiting for a relationship with a difference. He wanted to have kids as well but saw no point in bringing children into the world in the absence of a covenant union - marriage.

"I hope you are not still expecting to have kids," I replied jokingly.

He laughed, released his hug and we walked back to the car so he could take me home. He turned the key and started the car but I felt that I should tell him about my encounter with God.

"You know, Harold, I have been paying close attention to André and his commitment to God. I truly believe that God sent him here to show me the way. Though I felt that his way of life was way too intense, André has taught me what Christianity means. Yesterday when I got home from the hospital I had an encounter with Jesus."

As I called His Name I felt His touch again and I began to cry. Harold turned off the engine and prayed encouragingly with me as I worshipped God for a brief moment.

"I cannot understand all of it yet, but I am sure that Jesus visited me in my room. I am as confident about it as I was about the reality of the vision. I know that this holy presence that is engulfing me, is God."

Harold was deeply moved and thanked God with me for the experience. We then drove home. My emotions were difficult to explain but I felt safe, clean, calm, tolerant, peaceful, worry-free, and most of all, I felt loved. Loved by God and loved by this special man. I silently thanked God for all that He had done for me.

Harold stayed the entire evening with us. We just 'chilled out' together and talked about all sorts of things. I watched my family and marveled at what God had done – I was just waiting for God to ask me to do something. I was not trying to repay Him; I knew I could never do that but I wanted to give back to society, to help someone. I had a little money and some skills and I vowed to keep asking Him to give me an assignment – I was going to give God everything. I was so grateful to Him, I felt as though I had the strength to do anything. I just wanted do something in return.

Harold had finally gotten a call to update him on the case. As he listened you could see the trepidation on his face; we wondered what in the world he was being told – it looked very serious. When he got off, we waited anxiously for him to share the news with us. He informed us that after a thorough search of the house and property where Andy had been kept, the police found skeletal remains of two bodies hidden in a very small make-shift basement under the structure.

Pictures, newspaper clippings and other items found at the house suggested that the remains were that of sixteen-year-old twin boys who had gone missing a little over two years before; the identities were unconfirmed. However, Gerard confessed to sodomizing and murdering the boys and to kidnapping and abusing Anderson. He was going to be charged with the offences the following day. Harold was almost certain that there would not be a preliminary inquiry nor a long drawn out trial as long as Gerard pleaded guilty – just a sentencing.

No trial was a good thing since Andy would have been a public spectacle if there were a trial. It then hit me that I was still being pretentious about my life. I had to be careful not to continue to give a false representation of who I was but to be truthful in all things. André said something earlier that had me thinking; he said that sometimes God allows things to happen so that our lives could be a testimony and that someone else could be helped by our experiences. I found that to be quite intriguing; maybe that was the thing that God wanted me to do – the assignment that I had begged for may very well include my testimony of deliverance and I could inspire other people. Interesting!

We were having a light dinner that night, we sat together at the family's dining table. I had insisted on this. No one objected as they too believed that the time we were spending together was beneficial to bonding. We had no real agenda but chatted on a variety of subjects and tried to come up with solutions to assist Andy with his emotional recovery when he came home from the hospital. I had no idea where it would take us that night but it turned out to be a time of sharing, confessions, openness, forgiveness and healing for my family.

Anton had not been out on a date since the episode with Princess. I still had all his money so he could not go anyway. He explained that he was getting a little frustrated. We truly felt for him but we were not about to be too accommodating though because a multiplicity of sex partners is an extremely dangerous undertaking and he needed to know that he should stop this irresponsible behaviour.

"I need some help too," he began honestly, as we listened attentively.

"Seriously, I don't sleep around because I want to. Sex is the only thing that relieves the tremendous pressure that builds up in me sometimes."

As he spoke, it occurred to me, "George did the same. We must help Anton or else he would destroy himself and anyone else who came into his life."

"After all we've been through this weekend, I need to go on a date. Well it's not a date I need, I need to have sex; I don't want to, I need to."

"Only God can break that hold, Anton," André suggested. "Your need should be God, not a woman. No wonder you told us you felt like an abuser, and I am not judging you – you already judged yourself and that's a good thing. You are right. I believe that God Himself allowed you to see it. You have to trust and believe God for deliverance from this habit. It could kill you."

"Deliverance sounds like what I need," he began, as his voice quivered and tears flowed. "But how, André, h-h-how!"

His emotions ran high and for the first time we saw Anton break and he sobbed bitterly. André went over to him and hugged him as he prayed to God for deliverance. Harold joined them and they both ministered to André as we sat agreeing with them in prayer.

It seemed like God had His plan and one by one, we were all examining ourselves and letting God in, slowly but surely. Anthony was quiet as usual and very supportive of what was taking place. The Spirit of God was strong in our house; but God was not finished with us yet. In fact, He had just gotten started. We stayed at the dinner table for hours that night. It was truly a night - of soul searching and getting real.

Sonja shared her testimony of how God had delivered her as well. She said she had been without a boyfriend because she could not handle breakups well at all. She was so hard to please that relationships just did not work out. Whenever she had a breakup or was under pressure she would drink. She always did it at home and fell asleep afterwards, but it was alcohol abuse none-the-less. No one really knew what was happening to her – she would be normal in the day but drank at night. Two years ago God arrested her. Sonja was dating Martin, one of the Deacons at her church. While on a date, he told her something that really upset her though he was right on target.

Their relationship ended that night, but before he did, he told her that he found her to be into herself to a degree that she could not love anyone unless they conformed to her. He also told her that she needed to yield to God fully if she ever wanted to be free from herself – a self-made prison. She did not take the speech too well and their date was cut short. He took her home. Tragically, he was killed fifteen minutes later by a drunk driver who broke a red light. His mother called her later that night with the news.

"My first inclination was to drink, but God took hold of me that night. Martin had hit the nail on the head when he told me of my character flaw. I knew he was right but I was stubborn. I broke when his mother called me. It was as if he had fulfilled his purpose in life and God had taken him home. I could not think. I was numb but conscious enough to pray. I then felt a presence in the room and suddenly I saw myself as though I was watching a movie. I knew that God had visited me. I began to cry - bawl I should say. I would have consumed that entire bottle of wine so that I could sleep that night but Holy Spirit said, "NO!" He showed me where I was not walking according to His will and His way. I prayed and worshipped God from my heart, and then I felt like I did not need the alcohol at all. I walked to the liquor cabinet as if on auto pilot and took every bottle of alcohol and poured it down in the kitchen sink. That was it. I did not hear God's voice audibly but He spoke to me that night; you know, that still small voice. His Spirit bore witness with my spirit and I was delivered."

You could hear the faint whispers of praises to God across the table. Everyone was in awe at the Mighty God we serve. I then told them of my experience with God and had André jumping and shouting loudly because his prayers had been answered and mission accomplished. This was our time! Jesus has the power to draw men unto Him for salvation and deliverance and He drew me. André could not stop and as the saying goes, 'If you can't beat them, join them'. We joined in the praises with him, giving thanks to God Almighty for His greatness. He then went to the piano and added music to our celebration with the moving hymn that will never get old, 'My Tribute', by Andrae Crouch.

How can I say thanks for the things
You have done for me
Things so underserved,
yet You gave to prove Your love for me
The voices of a million angels
cannot express my gratitude
All that I am and ever hope to be, I owe it all to Thee
To God be the Glory, To God be the Glory,
To God be the Glory
For the things He has done
With His blood, He has saved me
With His power He has raised me
To God be the Glory
For the Things He has done

Harold took the second verse, his baritone voice echoing into our spirits ...

Just let me live, my life
Let it be pleasing Lord to Thee
And should I gain, any praise
Let it go to Calvary
With His blood, He has saved me
With His power He has raised me
To God be the Glory
For the Things He has done.

Glory to God; that was a moment to savour – basking in God's presence as He descended from His throne in the heavens and into my home – a home that was once filled with pride, anger, hatred, abuse and humiliation, was transformed into a House of Praise. We all joined the contagiously captivating melody and sang the chorus with them.

To God be the Glory, To God be the Glory,
To God be the Glory
For the things He has done
With His blood, He has saved me
With His power He has raised me
To God be the Glory
For the Things He has done

Tears filled our eyes. We spent a few more minutes hugging each other, forgiving one another and promising to stick together as a family should. I thought that my kids were too old and that all was lost but I guess that God had the final say on that one. It was not too late. Life had new meaning – real meaning. Blessed be the name of the Lord.

We were getting a little hungry again so we made sandwiches and a fruit punch. We were not done yet; this family had a lot more to talk about. Harold thought it was time to tell them that we were officially a couple. As he made the announcement, Sonja could have reached the roof with excitement but I was especially appreciative of how much my sons wanted me to have a male companion, someone of significance in my life. Their comments made me blush and then they started to jeer. I am good for myself, you know, and so I fired back wittily causing them all to laugh hilariously.

"Listen, gentlemen. Don't think for even a fleeting moment that because I now have a man in my life that I won't be in yours. You better know that for sure, I am mother; we did not choose each other. Someone else had a say in that, and so I will always be mother, regardless of how much man you feel you are."

We shared a good laugh as Harold placed his hand across my shoulders, further reassuring me of his love.

My sons are adults so he told them like it is; how he would take care of me and would respect me at all times. He also sort of lectured to all of us on the importance of trust and honesty in any relationship and promised my family that he would never put me through anything that resembled the trauma that I had been through. Though they still did not know the severity of the situation, they knew that I had gone through what I considered hell, with George.

Our fellowship continued way into the night, as we jumped from topic to topic. Somewhere along the line, the topic of abortion came up. We discussed our views on how devastating abortion really is.

"It is murder. No one should deny that," said André, whose views were extremely strong. "The laws that they are trying to pass are going to have grave consequences for this nation. We need to stand up against it."

I myself had been following the developments and added, "That is really true; pretty soon, if the law is passed a fifteen-year-old girl can have an abortion without even telling her parents that she is pregnant. I wonder whom will they contact if complications occur. The abortionist had better take care of that child. As far as I'm concerned, if the Government says that she does not need to tell me anything, they had better be prepared to care for her afterward should problems arise and not burden me financially or emotionally, though we really cannot escape the emotional trauma."

Not everyone at the table was comfortable talking about abortion and it began to show. It was as though the night was too perfect to be true and there just had to be something that would attempt to spoil it. André and Aphelia had an open fight that shocked us beyond belief. We did not even think that it was possible for those two to argue since their love seemed to be as secure and as sure as there was a yesterday. It started when Sonja and Aphelia began to fuss softly, then it became loud enough to cause each of us to stop our own little conversations and pay attention.

"Mom, I have to do this."

"Yes, you do, but not now," replied Sonja. She was firm.

Aphelia did not obey her mother and just turned to André. He had no clue as to what was coming and it hit him in a sore spot; he was surprised and unable to control his temper for a moment.

"When I got to New York after we broke up," she began, "I found out that I was pregnant. I..."

He raised his hands, bowed his head and stopped her. His eyes widened and he sat up straight. He wanted to believe that she had lost the baby naturally but that was not the case.

"Pregnant! You had a miscarriage?" asked André, though I was sure he knew the answer to that.

"No, I had an abortion."

The topic of abortion stirred Aphelia's spirit and she evidently felt guilty that her wedding was two weeks away and her husband-to-be had no clue that she had aborted his child.

"You had an abortion?" he repeated incredulously, sitting back in the chair and looking a little angry and a lot disappointed in the choice that Aphelia had made.

"André, that was a long time ago."

"How in God's name could you do something like that?

Aunty Sonja, how could you allow her to do that?"

"Don't lose respect for me, André," replied Sonja. She was a tough one, André should have known better.

"Sorry, Aunty, I did not mean to disrespect you. I just don't understand this."

"What did you want me to do, André?" said Aphelia trying very hard to hold back the tears.

"Aphelia, we were clear on what we would do if you did get pregnant." His voice became a little louder; Aphelia did not like that at all.

"Please, don't raise your voice at me," she demanded. "I was clear on what our plans were as well, but that did not happen. You changed the plans - you are the one that broke up with me – I did not ask for that."

"What does that have to do with having an abortion?"

"Everything!" she replied, wondering if he had forgotten that he did hurt her dreadfully with the unexpected breakup.

"Aphee, have you even considered the consequences? I want kids but do you know if you can get pregnant again, and what about the spiritual complications?"

This was going a little too far - Sonja and I eyed each other, thinking that we may need to intervene. We decided however to let them trash it out for themselves. Let them vent. In that atmosphere venting was healthy.

"I had no intentions of bringing a child into this world to grow up like me. No offense, Mother, but I did not want a fatherless child."

"Is that what you thought of me, Aphelia?"

"André, at that time I did not know what to think."

"Come on, you know me better than that," he said, sounding a little angrier than before.

Aphelia was breaking at this point. She folded her arms across her chest and looked him directly into his eyes. "I thought I did know you, André, but that was before you left me."

André got up and grabbing his car keys and cell phone, he replied without moving his eyes off her gaze.

"Can't change the past. This is a pointless argument – I need some air." He walked to the back door. Aphelia called after him, "André, please!"

He lifted his hands as if to say: I hear you, but not now. Aphelia was hurt – she did not know what had happened. She cried, obviously concerned as to what would become of them now. She wondered if they should have waited instead of planning to get married so soon after their reunion. But then she was also confident of God's leading and knew that it was no mistake.

"Aunt Mel, don't let André leave, please."

"He will not go anywhere sweetie. It's late."

"I should have listened to you, Mother," she cried uncontrollably

"I'll go talk to him, okay." I got up to follow André.

Sonja was kind of angry with Aphelia because she had told her to wait. She hugged her but had a few harsh words for her as well: "You young people feel you know everything; that's why God gave you parents. I told you not to say anything now."

"Mother, he had to know and I wanted to be honest. It was killing me."

"I know he should know, Aphelia, but you must choose the time and the place. Your timing was totally off, and the place – you cannot discuss something as sensitive as this in front of everybody."

I heard Sonja's advice to her daughter as I left to get André. She is a very smart woman. André really did not go anywhere but was sitting on the bench in the backyard. I sat beside him.

"Son, why did you get so angry?"

"I don't know! I felt she should have told me about that as soon as she came back."

"Tell me something. Would that have made a difference? Even if you knew before, would you not still marry her?"

"Yes, I would - I won't take it that far."

"Then stop acting like a spoilt child and as if you never make mistakes. Go in there and talk to her," I said, lifting my voice a tad higher than before. "André, this is what, the first fight in two weeks; if you guys don't fight then I will begin to worry. Don't prolong this any longer. Stop blaming Aphelia; you left her hurt and confused – remember that."

Without any protest he followed my advice and went back inside. As the door opened Aphelia turned around, her tear-stained face a little puffy from crying. André walked up to her and hugged her, and apologised for his outburst. I wondered if it was possible to settle issues so easily, but I guess they would have to talk about that in a lot more detail in private. I told them what I thought of the whole thing because it was obvious to me that they had spent all their time falling in love all over again and not dealing with the previous hurt. I felt that they should take some time to deal with it, talk about how they felt when they broke up and what they expected from each other now; then forgive and move on. I wondered how it is that I could not have given myself such smart advice when I was hurting. *Forgive*, I actually used the word *forgive* and yet I still had not forgiven totally. I knew that I had to and I would, but not right away. Unbelievably, even after my experience, I still felt that it was my right to withhold forgiveness for certain things.

Anthony was basically silent the entire evening, he did not share anything significant with us. Except to say that he was glad he stayed around. I could hardly wait for the day he opened up.

Harold got up; it was time to go home. It was already 11:30 p.m. and he had to work the following day. Time well spent, it did not feel like so many hours at all. I walked him to the door – his hand in mine. He again told me how much he loved me, hugged me once more, kissed my cheek and promised to call the following day. When I got back into the dining room everyone else was getting ready to turn in for the night. We bade each other good night. André and Aphelia, however, remained downstairs just as we expected. Communication is extremely important in all relationships.

That was a day that I would forever remember. Everything was orchestrated in such a way that brought an immeasurable amount of happiness and joy to me. I knew without a doubt that God was in it all. I was beginning to sound like André. How could I not? I only then understood a little of what he had been telling me all along.

Sonja went upstairs with me and we sat in my room for a little while longer. No raised voices downstairs so we assumed that the love birds were conversing in a decent manner. I told her in detail the experience I had had the day before and we spent some time in prayer. She read portions of the Bible that helped me to understand my new walk in Christ. Firstly, she opened to the book of John and read the famous verse sixteen of chapter three:

> *"For God so loved the world that He gave His only begotten son, that whosoever believeth in Him should not perish but have everlasting life."*

She also continued to the seventeenth verse:

> *"For God did not send His son into the world to condemn the world but that the world through Him might be saved."*

Sonja said that it was important that I did not feel condemned because I was now set free. She turned to II Corinthians 5:17,

> *"Therefore if any man be in Christ he is a new creation; old things are passed away and all things are become new."*

"God made you over, Mel, a new person; the old Mel is gone, washed in the blood of Jesus."

"It's amazing how I feel white as snow though washed in His blood. Isn't blood red?"

"Jesus' saving power is miraculous."

Sonja pointed to other scriptures that gave me answers to burning questions and told me to start reading the book of John and the Psalms. The gospel of John, she explained was important for me to further comprehend who Jesus is and why salvation is important.

She went to bed and I also fell asleep, feeling light and loved and wondering - What next? What does my God have in store for me? I was eager to start my new life – Life in Jesus – and life with a new boyfriend, Harold. Everything was happening so fast I felt like God catapulted my life forward to compensate for some of the hurt I endured; a drastic move from over twenty years of abuse to fun-filled freedom in two weeks!

Chapter Nine

The wedding day arrived. The men, including Anderson, were at Anthony's apartment. The other groomsmen would join them later as they all were dressing there. We wanted to be a little bit traditional and not let André see Aphelia until she walked up the aisle.

Anderson had been home for almost two weeks and was recovering nicely. He was in good enough shape to be a groomsman, though not fully recovered yet. There were times when he would be alone and days that he did not even leave his room but we kept close watch and looked for signs of suicide and depression. Sonja had contacted Dr. Matthews. Anderson had met with him four times already and was scheduled to visit twice per week for the next two months. I had decided to take care of him myself for a while so he did not have to bother with working just yet. Sonja and I prayed together daily and Anderson was definitely on top of the list. I learned a lot from those sessions.

Aphelia was up early. She dressed at my home along with all of her bridesmaids. They opted for an afternoon wedding and the reception and dance were scheduled to follow immediately. In Trinidad and

Tobago one cannot get married after 6:00 p.m. so though they wanted to celebrate all night long, we had to commence the wedding by four o'clock. Harold had been more than a blessing. In addition to offering them the restaurant, and doing the catering, he and his staff organised the entire décor which was a huge load off our shoulders. We had no clue what it looked like but trusted him to come up with something spectacular.

The house was full of activity: two hairdressers and a make-up specialist were working tirelessly to make six beautiful young ladies and two gorgeous grown women even more glamorous. I felt as if I was living in an unending fairytale. Sonja and I were giving away our children together – Aphelia insisted on not choosing any man to be father giver. Sonja had been mother and father in her life so regardless of what tradition said, she wanted her mother to walk her up the aisle and hand her to André.

The church was fifteen minutes away and so we had the limousines pick us up at 3:30p.m. We were so excited! André called to say that he had forgotten to take the rings with him and told me where to get them. I got the rings and tucked them away safely in my purse. It was time to go and everyone looked really great. Aphelia began to cry. The photographer and the cosmetologist quickly calmed her down because she would have ruined her make-up. She was so overcome with joy but pulled herself together.

When we reached the church the men were already there and waiting. Proudly, I looked at my four sons – the most handsome in all the earth. God could not have done a better job. An usher signaled that it was time to begin and everyone took their positions. Anthony and I stood next to André in front of the podium at the centre of the church.

The ceremony began – the groomsmen were sitting in the front row and as the music played they left their positions and walked slowly down the aisle to meet the bridesmaids at the entrance of the church. They presented each of them with a lovely bouquet of red roses. They then proceeded up the aisle in slow steady steps to the tune of an instrumental by Kenny Rogers. The bridesmaids dresses were predominantly gold with a hint of champagne and their feet were clad in gold toned shoes with straps covered in rhinestones. The groomsmen wore black tuxedos with a black and gold trimmed vest and bow tie. I saw everyone but my eyes were fixed on Anderson – he looked fantastic as he walked with Aphelia's cousin. No one could tell that he had been through a life-altering ordeal recently.

The bridesmaids and the groomsmen were in place, lining the front of the church. It was time for the bride to come in. Pastor Joseph's five-year-old daughter was the flower girl. Accompanied by another young boy from his church, who was probably about five years old as well, they preceded the bride carrying the rings on a pillow and sprinkling flowers on the red carpet. They took their positions and the Pastor asked that all stand – the bride was coming.

They did not choose the popular bridal march but opted for the very song that André used as background music for his dramatic proposal: 'Endless Love'. She dazzled the guests as she slowly walked up the aisle with her mother at her side. André's face was alight with joy though he shook a little nervously beside me.

Aphelia chose not to wear a white dress – we honoured her choice. She wore a long sleeved, champagne-coloured dress, fitted down to her knees then finishing with a fish-tailed skirt. The trail was about eight feet long and adorned with rich appliqués and pearl beads. The top of the dress featured a deep 'V' neckline. It was the first time I had seen a little cleavage; I was not even sure if you could call that cleavage. She had her hair rolled up and wore a tiara. She smiled at the guests as she walked slowly up the aisle. André met her just before the podium and took her from her mother's arm. He then walked with her, arm in arm, as they completed the journey to the altar to be married. I had been to a number of weddings but this moment was breathtaking. This was my son – André was really getting married.

Before we knew it, the ceremony was over. The time came to present them for the first time as man and wife. Pastor Joseph had them face the congregation and said the magic words ...

"With the power invested in me, I now pronounce you man and wife. You may kiss your bride."

I don't know why people craved pictures of that kiss - it's just a kiss - but all the photographers, hired or not, began to fuss around to get into a good position to capture the event. André did not even look nervous anymore and he had to add some drama to it! He held her passionately then tilted her backwards as he bent forward and kissed her for what seemed like an entire minute. He could not care less; he had waited four years for that moment. The picture "take-outers" had definitely gotten something to snap.

The recessional took place pretty quickly and we accompanied the wedding party to take additional photographs at the Botanical Gardens. God had blessed us with a lovely day and so that venue was the perfect place for capturing the memories. The Botanical Gardens is famous for its luscious lawns, huge trees and richly coloured croton shrubs. It is often used by couples for their wedding photos and so we met two other weddings there.

At the reception hall, the guests were seated and waited patiently for the newlyweds, having chosen not to accompany us to the 'photo-shoot'. Harold had stayed at the hall to handle the activities there and so did not attend the church ceremony. On our arrival we were ushered to our seats and awaited the entry of the bride and groom. Sonja and I were in awe as we laid eyes on the décor. We could not have asked for anything more magnificent. When Harold stopped to greet us we told him how awed we were and thanked him for everything. He got the signal that they were ready and went to announce them. The live band played softly as André and Aphelia walked into the room. My brains could take no more excitement; it was full to capacity.

The evening moved along; the speeches, the sticking of the cake, the first dance - everything seemed to be just perfect. The dance floor was then opened and everyone who could find a partner jumped in. I noticed that Anderson had a few sets with Aphelia's cousin and he looked cool, calm and collected. Sonja met an old family friend and she too got up to dance. Harold was a little busy as he had done a lot for the wedding himself but he found the time and came and sat beside me.

"Hey, beautiful, heaven must be missing an angel because you are here."

I blushed slightly, not believing that overused line would make me blush. I was going to be fifty the following week, and I still blushed. Harold asked me to dance as Celine Dion's "Angel" started to play. We did not speak much at all while we danced but just enjoyed each other's company. The newlyweds then left the reception and made their way back home. They were leaving for St. Thomas early the next morning and would return on Friday. We all went home shortly afterwards; it had been a wonderfully fulfilling day. Harold walked me to the limo, holding my hand.

"Did I tell you how absolutely marvelous you look tonight?"

"I don't think you did actually, so why don't you tell me."

"Mel, you look fantastic."

"Well, thank you, Harold."

"You're welcome."

It is so amazing to see how everyone needs love regardless of age. I was enjoying giggling romantically with Harold and saying a lot that really meant nothing at all and yet it still felt as good as it did when I was eighteen. Our relationship was growing pretty fast but as far as physical contact was concerned, we had kept that holy and did nothing to contradict the relationship that I was building with God - until that night. I thought about how it would feel if he kissed me – it seemed the natural thing to do as we professed our love for each other. I never asked for, nor prompted the event though, and neither did he. I could tell he wanted to though. I knew it would happen but I was not in a hurry.

I was about to get into the limo and turned to say a final goodbye when Harold just pulled me in and planted one – it took me by surprise. At first I allowed him. But then I did not feel what I thought I should. Instead that kiss woke up something in me that I did not want to remember. I pulled away and did not look at him or even say goodbye. I just got into the limo and closed the door. I could see him through the tinted glass.

He could no longer see me. He just stood there with his hands in his pockets. I watched him until the limo turned a corner. I wondered what was going through his mind.

When we got home I told Sonja what had happened and she was concerned that I, in fact, had not moved on and it was quite possible that I was harbouring hatred for men although Harold and I were doing so well. She reminded me that the relationship was almost as old as George's death, so I should take my time.

"Sonja, what on earth am I going to do? I love him. I'm sure of it."

"You must forgive the people that hurt you in the past or else you will live in defeat continuously, making others suffer for things that they did not do. Specifically, you must forgive George."

"I am aware that I must let go; it is not easy though."

"I know but God will help you through it."

We went to bed and when we got up the next day, Anthony had already taken André and Aphelia to the airport. I remembered the issue with Harold and decided to pray about that whole thing that morning. It sounded kind of silly at first, praying to God about a kiss; but somehow talking to God about everything seemed to be my newly-found, heart-yearning trend. Previously I talked to myself about everything but could find no answers and no peace; obviously, I am not God. Also, the kiss was definitely not the issue; I knew that for sure.

I was preparing to go to church with Sonja when my cell phone rang – it was Harold. It was only 8:15; I guess he could not wait any longer to talk about the situation.

"Hello," I answered quite casually, trying to pretend.

"Good morning, Mel," he said, equally as casual as I was. "I think I offended you last night. I am really very sorry. I must have misread the whole thing and I acted selfishly. But I care about you a lot and I thought the time was right." He did not beat around the bush but said what he needed to immediately.

"It's not you, Harold, it's me. I am probably not over the ordeal that my marriage turned out to be."

I sighed as if I had the world on my shoulders then told him that Sonja and I had planned to go to church so I had to get ready. I promised to call him after service and then he could pick me up and we would have lunch and discuss the matter.

My first full gospel church service since giving my heart to Christ was really enlightening. Anthony and Anderson had accompanied us and we did have a time in the presence of God. The church was vibrant, clapping, singing, rejoicing – it was amazing. When the preacher started to preach at first, I felt like André had told him our story though I knew that that was not true. His topic was on forgiveness. He was a visiting preacher - it was coincidental, but timely. The name of that amazing speaker was Apostle Duncan. He said that he was asked by Pastor Joseph to speak on Evangelism but God told him to talk about forgiveness and its effects on those who refuse to forgive. He respectfully asked Pastor Joseph's permission to 'follow God'. I got to thinking: if God speaks to people maybe He did speak to Apostle Duncan and told him what to say. I decided to listen to what was being preached and tried to internalize it and forgive, and so move on. I had honestly prayed and asked God to help me forgive and to help me get on with my life. This preacher was actually giving us step by step instructions. That was a first for me, and I knew in my heart that it was the answer to my prayers. Apostle Duncan had written a book on the topic, "Forgiveness Unlimited", and had a few copies with him that day. I bought one and promised to read it thoroughly to grasp the concepts.

A number of people responded to Apostle Duncan when he asked them if they needed to get over their unforgiving ways. The altar was full before I could get up and so I stayed in my seat. I was so glad I did since people were puking and crying and I could not understand what was happening. Sonja later explained that that was what happened when God delivered people from demonic possession.

As promised, when I got home I called Harold. He picked me up and we went to a Chinese Restaurant in Long Circular Mall for lunch. The restaurant had a cozy setting. Chinese paintings and artifacts were hung all around. We did not say anything much at all while we ate but I knew he wanted answers. We sat across from each other in one of the cushioned cubicles. I looked at him briefly wondering what on earth I was going to say to him. I continued my lunch. He could no longer remain quiet.

"Mel,"

I looked up again. *Oh God, help! What do I do - what do I say?*

"You need to know that I did not mean to upset you last night."

"I know that, Harold. My issues really have nothing to do with you."

"Oh, but it does, because it is affecting me – us – this

relationship."

I thought maybe I should give up on having a relationship because I was hoping to feel something move inside me or I would see some bright light or something, but nothing happened.

"Listen, maybe you should find someone who is ready for intimacy."

Harold could not believe his ears; but I did not know what else to say. His mouth opened, his jaw dropped. He acted like he was in a state of shock; he sat up straight.

"It was only a kiss, Melinda. Intimacy! Why would I ...?"

I bowed my head, a little bit ashamed of my comment and suffering from 'can I do this?'

"Look at me, Melinda," he lovingly demanded and I obeyed. "I am not looking for anything more right now."

"Well, I don't know when or if I'll ever be ready."

"Then I'll wait!" he said beginning to sound a tad frustrated. "I have been waiting and I will continue to do so."

"Well, you can't wait forever."

"Oh yeah, watch me."

"What do you really want from me; what exactly are you expecting?"

"Nothing in particular - nothing before its time and definitely nothing that displeases God. I just want to be with you. But what is this; I don't understand why you're even talking like this?"

I still hoped to feel something that could give me a

sign from God as to whether or not I should continue this relationship. I felt nothing, I thought it meant to give it up – stay alone for the rest of my life.

"I don't know if I can do this. I saw George last night. You kissed me but I saw George, ripping through me and taking my life away."

I began to get somewhat emotional so he changed his position and sat beside me. He held my hands and I could not decipher what the look on his face meant. Was it concern, despair, fear of losing me? I could not tell.

"So what are you saying, Mel? I need to know because I am not George."

Harold clearly wanted me to be precise. He was not about to guess what the future held for us

"I don't want to hold you back from having a fulfilling life."

"Okay; that's enough! Hold me back? Have you any clue how long I waited for this? I merely tried to express my love. I know what you've been through; I know you need time - I will help you through it. I'm not in a hurry. I understand that you may not be ready and I will wait. I was careful not to act like a typical 'man'. So tell me please, what have I done to be treated like this? It's as though you're pushing me away now."

I was unresponsive. I did not know what to do. George still had power over me. I was not grieving for him; in fact, I was glad that he had died. His death was not a factor in my life at all. We had been going through the motions; George was dead to all of us a long time ago. The situation was so devastating it was as though George was just someone we knew, yet his evil face surfaced whenever I thought of anything concerning sex

167

– even a kiss. Harold disturbed my thoughts: "Mel, I have always shown you the ultimate respect. Please don't turn away from me – give it a try."

I honestly did not have an answer for him; I was just scared as hell to even think that I could be with a man again. I was prepared to live like a cloistered nun if I had to. However, I tried to let my mind focus on the facts and not feelings.

"I'm sorry I kissed you, Mel. I will ask your permission next time. You know what, if we are going to be together, I should be able to freely kiss you at some point, don't you think?"

"And how long will you be willing to wait for that?"

Harold stared into my eyes and did not answer. He then caressed my face softly, holding the deafening stare – I guessed he decided to let his eyes do the talking instead but he wanted a response. I slowly began to feel comfortable with him again, and did not mind his touching my face. My heart was beating so fast I swore my blood pressure rose. We've been together only a few weeks, I reminded myself. How long do I wait? When will it be right? I could not answer any of those questions. I had not kissed George for many years – did I even remember how? I kept thinking. I loved Harold and was sure of it. I agreed to be with him so I should not let him pay George's tab. I will try again. I should allow him to kiss me. It took a little while but I eventually responded to him by holding his elbow but still he said nothing. We looked at each other for a while still, each thinking our own thoughts.

"I love you." he whispered, then waited for me to respond. I wanted to know if I could. I needed to know if I was normal. I had prayed and asked God to help me forgive and move on. Maybe this was moving on; Harold should not have to ask my permission, I'll be messing with his ego. I decided to go for it and bravely responded.

"I love you, too; you may kiss me again." He leaned forward and stopped just inches from my lips. My heart raced but I wanted to move on with my life; I refused to let my negative past define my future.

"Are you sure?" his whisper even softer than before...

"I'm sure."

He completed the journey to my lips – my eyes wandered, but I did not see George's evil face again. He kept one hand across my shoulders and with the other gently lifted my chin. What was probably a few seconds felt like five minutes. The moment was beautiful; I loved it and felt secure. I had jumped one hurdle I suppose, but only God knew at that point if I could jump the other; we were no way near that stage in any event. He returned to his seat opposite me. We had not finished eating yet.

"Are you alright?" he asked, flashing a satisfied smile on his face - his dimples sinking deep into his cheek bone.

"I'm still breathing. I think I'm just fine."

"Thank you."

"For what?"

"Thank you for allowing me to love you. You could have easily closed up on me and ended the relationship, but you are loosening the knots now, I can tell. You certainly scared me today."

"I scared you?" I did not even think that I was making him feel insecure at all. I thought he was way too strong for that.

"Yeah, for a moment there I thought it was over."

Harold knew full well that I was not really scared of kissing but rather what the kiss could lead to. We talked about sex and he reassured me that he was following the guidelines for Christian living. The boundaries were set by God and he would not even consider any sexual contact outside of marriage. We both knew what sin was and purposed to steer clear from it. He was not oblivious to his sexuality though.

"Melinda, I am human but I would go home and shower in ice if I have to. I promise you that I will never put you in a position to sin against God."

"But doesn't kissing lead to sex?"

"Yes, if it is prolonged, but not a smack that says I love you – not to mention in public."

Harold was probably right. I was happy that we had that conversation. I should have known though because we were this close before and he never stepped out of line.

"I believe that it is my duty to maintain respect in this relationship," he continued. "Notice carefully, when I take you out to dinner, I take you home afterwards. I have never invited you to my place. It's not because I feel nothing for you but because God has given me the strength to obey His commands. If we create an atmosphere conducive for sexual activities, the human side of me will respond to that and I know that it would be difficult to control it."

"But you come to my house."

"I feel safe there - your kids and Sonja are around. I

won't disrespect them either. There is no one at my house. We must shun the very appearance of evil and give no room for the devil to operate. In addition to all this, Mel, I know that you are definitely not ready to indulge in sex. All that would do is destroy you completely. I love you too much to allow that to happen."

"Seems like you actually thought about all of this."

"I have to. Seeing you again brought back memories of the intense feelings we had for each other years ago. We could not act on it then, but what's to stop us now? God must be preserving us for something spectacular because we are together now and we are saved, so we still cannot act on it... but God's timing is perfect."

I couldn't help thinking: I have gotten the last of the best men. Women persistently complain about men who fail to show, or are not competent to show how much they care. Some men only blurt out the sacred words, 'I love you', in a fit of ecstasy. At that point one must wonder if they love the person or the activity.

"I feel privileged to be your girlfriend. If more people thought like you there would be so much less pain."

"I have learned my lesson. I do not play the dating game at all."

"What do you mean by that?"

"I made up my mind to wait until I felt that nudge in my spirit; until I felt like God said, 'Good choice; go for it'. I had no intentions of getting involved with anybody unless I believe it would lead to marriage."

"Is that a proposal?" I teased him, causing him to blush now. Oh look at that, even tough Harold could blush.

"Not yet," he replied smiling. "But I do want you to

know that I am not playing games."

Harold's position on dating was serious. He said that too many people, Christians in particular, get caught up with physical attraction and find themselves in sin. Too many dates are based purely on emotions - they start kissing, touching, heavy petting and for some, sex. It is sinful, and it hurts badly if the relationship doesn't work out. Worst yet, those choices form ungodly soul ties. Many who get caught up in it also go through a hurricane of guilty feelings. Holy Spirit won't let up, constantly convicting of sin. It winds up affecting their relationship with God, thus also hampering our main purpose on earth – fulfilling the Kingdom of God – winning souls for Christ and doing His will.

"We need to guard ourselves against sin and make certain to please God always." Harold was pretty firm in his belief and I wondered about his relationship with Evelyn. Did he treat her this way? Even so, I knew they broke up before he had changed. But how special was she? I wondered.

"What kind of relationship did you have with Evelyn, if you don't mind me asking?"

"Not at all, no secrets, right? We had a good relationship – it was sexual. She practically lived at my house. Then I found out who she really was." He told me the whole story - the experience that had him running to Christ. Why do we wait for trauma to call on God? Man is so full of himself and thinks that he can make it on his own. Can't anyone just serve God without being beckoned by disaster? I hoped no one was hearing my thoughts because I was chief at trying to do it on my own.

Evelyn was a Grenadian national who had moved to Trinidad when she was twenty-eight years old. She had lied to Harold about her life and he never knew that she was a married woman with two children. Eventually, after many years, her husband came looking for her and found her at Harold's house. They had already been living together for three years. Like a typical man, not knowing the lies his wife had told, he attacked Harold. He fought back but then Evelyn's husband pulled a gun so he stopped struggling and focused on preserving his life. The man knocked him out with the gun butt and he stripped him of Evelyn, his jewelry, clothing, collectibles and a few thousand dollars that he had at the house.

He did not go to the police. He speculated on the theory that maybe Evelyn herself had set him up. He had asked Evelyn to marry him more than once but she came up with good excuses why she could not at the time. They had gotten engaged but of course could not get married since she was already married. Evelyn called him about a month later but as soon as he recognised her voice he hung up. She never tried contacting him again. That was four years ago. He was still skeptical about women – afraid to trust, afraid to love, until we had reconnected.

"I have not been in any real relationship since; I waited for the right person to come along. I honestly did not want to get close to someone again without the assurance that it was forever. In my search for true love, I found Jesus – Love Himself."

"You told me you went on a date about eight months ago, didn't you?"

"Yeah, but that was just once. I took this lady to dinner. She got a call while we ate and I did not like the manner in which she spoke to whoever she was speaking to. I mean pure ghetto – the language she used was deplorable. I called a taxi to take her home and left."

"You did not even take her home?"

"I did not even finish eating."

"Oh my Lord, Harold!" I said thinking that I should be on my "P's and Q's".

"Melinda, I was already saved. I really had no business dating a woman who did not know God anyway. The Bible calls that being unequally yoked."

"But you do realise that you made a commitment to me before I told you of my salvation experience."

"I knew before you told me. The nudge - I got it. Besides, our whole experience is different, and, you are really not a stranger to me."

I did know Harold for a long time and I knew how much he respected women. Our relationship years ago was tense. We tried to hide our feelings but they were rather powerful. I pulled away and he did the same. He met Evelyn and started bringing her to Anne's. I remember being jealous but could do nothing. Then I stopped going to Anne's. I had not seen Harold for about six years or so.

He took me home after our enlightening discussion. We sat in the car for a few minutes. The next thing he said to me was like a spiritual revelation. He switched off the engine. There was a look of sincerity in his eyes as he said, "Melinda Graham, I love you. The Bible says that all things work together for good. I have no doubt in my mind that the events of the past few weeks were all signs of God working out everything for our good. There is not another man on the face of this earth that will treat you the way that I will. All the mistakes we made in the past are nullified because God has placed our sins in the sea of forgetfulness. He remembers them no more but we remind Him daily. I am not perfect and neither are you – but I love you and I want you to be my wife. I know that I must wait and I will for as long as it takes. I will not hurt you deliberately – and if I do hurt you I will make sure to set things right swiftly. I will love your kids and grandkids like they are mine. I will embrace your dreams and aspirations like they are mine. I will keep God first in my life always and strive to be like Jesus – the Author and Finisher of our faith. With God all things are possible."

I opened my mouth to answer but he placed his fingers on my lips, "Don't say a word, just think about what I said – I mean it."

Harold did not come in but left immediately to go to his own house. It was only then I realised I had no clue where he lived; it had never dawned on me to even ask.

"Selfish woman," I rebuked myself and thought that I would definitely ask some pertinent questions the next time we saw each other.

My mind quickly went back to his speech. His words were very encouraging. If I did not love him before I loved him now for sure.

Chapter Ten

y fiftieth birthday was approaching swiftly, and I decided to have a small party at home. Sonja was booked on a flight for July 7th, so I decided to throw her a going away party at the same time. I remembered being very tired on the Friday before the party. We were busy that entire week but our activities, though tiring, were not burdensome. They included taking Andy to Gerard's place to retrieve his belongings, and accompanying him to Dr. Matthews' office. He was doing fine; he had told me that he was ready to work but I begged him to stay at home for a while longer. We kept in contact with Keith who also called to check on Andy from time to time.

I was folding laundry in my room when Andy came in to see me. We talked for a while then he told me that he was going to hang out with Keith that night but I had apprehensions: "I don't think that's a good idea, Andy."

"Mom, I am fine."

"Yes son, I see that you are but I would like you to relax a little longer."

"I will not stay like a prisoner in this house, Mom."

I began to get a little concerned about the direction this conversation was going, I asked him to sit so that we could talk freely. "Andy, are you trying to get out of a homosexual lifestyle?"

"Yes, that is what Dr. Matthews and I are dealing with."

"Great, then you must stay away from anything that can draw you back into it."

"I understand, Mom, but Keith is no longer homosexual. Remember? He got out as well and he helps me."

"I know but ..."

I stopped. I wanted to set Anderson free but I was really very scared to do so. I also did not want to control him either.

"Where are you planning to go?"

"Movie Towne."

"Will anyone else be going?"

"Yeah, a group of us are going actually, I will ask Anton to go with us as well if that will make you feel more comfortable."

"Please do. I'm sorry for treating you like a child but ..."

"Don't apologise! I understand and I appreciate everything that you are doing for me right now. If it were not for you, God knows."

I smiled as he turned and walked away silently thanking God for his humility. I was expecting André and Aphelia soon. Anthony had gone to the airport to pick them up. Sonja was getting her stuff together as she prepared to leave the following Tuesday. That period of my life was filled with emotions. I felt as though I had lived my whole life in a month; everything significant had happened in those few weeks. What was I doing for all of my life I wondered? I was beginning to think that I was not only given a second chance, but an entirely new life.

I had not seen Harold since the Sunday before. I picked up the phone to call him just to say hello - you know, the love sick teenager who must just call her boyfriend. Will I ever get over this period? "Hi Harold, what's up?"

"I'm good, how are you?"

"I'm doing fine."

We chatted for a little while then I heard voices and knew that André and Aphelia were back from their honeymoon.

"The lovebirds just returned."

"Okay, I'll talk to you later then."

He was sort of abrupt and it suddenly dawned on me that it seemed like he was a little uninterested in seeing or talking to me that week.

"Are you coming over later, Harold?"

"No I can't come over. I have to be at the restaurant tonight."

"Okay, so when am I seeing you next?"

"Sunday, your birthday party, remember."

"Of course, I remember."

"Great, I'll see you then, okay."

"Okay, bye."

He hung up and I could not help but wonder just a little. He had been around so frequently over the past few weeks that it was strange that he had not been there at all for that week. I tried not to think about it too much but concentrated on my family and the 50th birthday bash.

Nightfall came in quickly. Anton and Andy did go to Movie Towne; André and Aphelia went in early and so Sonja, Anthony and I were left; we decided to watch a movie. I looked at the clock; it was ten o'clock and Andy had not come home yet. Anthony said that the night was young still and not to worry. But I did worry and I came up with a ridiculous idea.

"Let's go to Movie Towne for ice-cream."

"Mom," said Anthony, "we are doing no such thing; leave him alone."

"Mel, you cannot watch this child forever. Chill!" insisted Sonja.

I knew they were right and tried to calm down. Not long afterwards we heard footsteps. Andy walked in the door – alone.

"Was the movie good?" I asked

"Yep," he replied, slumping into the chair next to us.

"Where's Anton?"

"There were girls at the movie, Mom."

He said that like I was supposed to know that Anton would pick up someone.

"Anton met a girl he knew since secondary school. He dropped me off then they went to Zen nightclub. I gave him cash and my credit card. Why doesn't he have any money?"

"I took away everything from him." Everyone looked at me like I was mad.

"What! He told me he was out of control and almost broke, he gave it up willingly. He is trying to get out of his addiction."

They stared even harder; no one commented at all though.

"All right, I'll give it back tomorrow."

I said nothing further. Anthony just burst out laughing and it just triggered the rest of us to laugh heartily too. I didn't really know if they were laughing at me or Anton but I really did not care.

I was a little disappointed to hear what Anton had done but my kids are grown. I was not concerned that he had gone out with a woman but that he would take her to a sleazy motel afterwards. I excused myself to go to the bathroom but also to call Harold; I had to get a little something off my chest. I dialed but he did not pick up. Why was I even considering this; he was probably busy for real. After all, he had a business to run? As I was heading back downstairs my phone rang; he was returning my call.

"Mel, is everything alright?" he asked a little concerned.

"Yes, I hope I did not worry you?"

"Not really. It's just kinda late and I thought you would be sleeping."

"No, we are watching a movie."

"Oh, okay. Well, why did you call?"

I was beginning to feel rather silly at that point, and only then realised that I really missed his company all week, so I decided to be honest.

"I miss you, Harold. I haven't seen you for the week."

"I miss you too."

"Well how come you did not try to see me these last few days?" He got it; he knew I was being childish and laughed at me.

"Did I spoil you rotten already?"

"I guess so," I began to laugh at myself now.

"I have a Manager on leave and two sick Supervisors so I had to stick around at the restaurant for longer periods. Maybe I should have told you but I did not think about it at all."

I breathed a small sigh of relief, stifling my breath as I didn't want him to hear it. I have no idea why it is so easy to assume the worst all the time.

"I'll take you for breakfast in the morning. How's that?

"Perfect."

"I love you, Mel"

Those words were as soothing as a cup of coffee in the morning.

"I love you too."

"Now go finish watching the movie and have a great

night, I'll see you in the morning."

Sonja was falling asleep on herself when I got back downstairs and Andy and Anthony were engulfed in the movie, "Armageddon", starring Bruce Willis, Liv Tyler and Ben Afleck. It was the first time that I had seen that movie although it was produced years ago. It reminded me about various types of love stories. Bruce's character reminded me of my father's love for me; Ben and Liv reminded me of Aphelia and André, crazy in love with each other and no one could come between them, and the saving-the-world bit reminded me of God's love for the people He created. We turned in after the movie. Anton had not yet come home but I reminded myself that he was a grown man and so I wouldn't lose sleep over him at all.

The next day everyone slept rather late. See what freedom does to you! When I watch the sun rise it is by choice as I relax in God's presence and not that I am burdened beyond reason. Harold called around 8:30 and asked if I was ready. I left the house before anyone else woke up. I did not even ask where he was taking me. He pulled into a gated community on Long Circular Road in St. James. We were having breakfast at his house – he had prepared it himself. It was so funny - one week ago I wondered how I had never even inquired as to where he lived and with whom and the next week I was there.

His two bedroom condominium was neatly organised and adorned with a few choice pieces of African figurines. The walls were painted in a soft yellow and the ceiling a deep gold. The living room only needed a few lengths of drapery and he chose a rich jacquard - a gold and maroon blend that matched perfectly with his décor. I wondered if a man could put away a house that well but he had decorated the restaurant himself and that was a work of art. I was certain most would believe that a woman had done it.

In the dining room was a small round table with just four chairs; we sat and enjoyed a hearty breakfast. He did not need to go out early that morning because the manager was scheduled to return to work that day. After breakfast, Harold let me into his life a little more as he showed me albums with pictures of his family and friends. His mother was still alive but his father had died a few years ago; he had three brothers and two sisters. The family was originally from Tobago - all of them, except Harold, still lived there. He promised to take me to Tobago some time to introduce me to them.

My cell phone rang; the caller ID revealed Anthony's number and I answered it. I had left the house before any one got up and so he wanted to know if all was well. Can you imagine that, my son is calling to check up on me? I was ready to go home - we were decorating the house that day for the party. But before we left, Harold said he had something for me. He went into the bedroom and came out with a beautifully wrapped gift.

"This is for you, my love. Happy Birthday!"

I was pleasantly surprised to say the least. "Thank you, but my birthday is tomorrow."

"I know that, but I do not want to wait till tomorrow. Open it." I hesitated a little, protesting that I liked to open birthday gifts on my birthday.

"Just open it, please!" Harold was very persistent.

I opened the package that was about two feet square. There were three boxes inside; in the first was an exquisitely, exorbitantly beautiful gown in my favourite colours – gold and red. I had not seen a more beautiful dress. I looked up at Harold and smiled; he too was smiling. The other box contained jewelry: a diamond and ruby necklace with matching earrings – I loved rubies, my birthstone. Finally, in the third box were shoes by Dolce and Gabana that matched with the jewelry. I felt extra special. I reached out and hugged him and thanked him for the gifts. He then asked me to try them on. I looked at him like he was a crazy person.

"I want you to wear it tomorrow - that is if you don't mind me planning your entire outfit."

I thought it was kinda cute but wondered how on earth he knew what sizes to buy. Sonja - it had to be Sonja. I went into his bedroom to try them on and could not help but notice how clean and serene he kept his entire house. I tried on the outfit and the shoes and everything fitted so well! I only had to make a little adjustment to the dress that I could have done myself. I did not let him see me in the dress; he would have to wait. I came out in the jeans and silk shirt that I was wearing. "You'll see me in these tomorrow for sure – they fit really well."

As I walked up to the porch I saw Anton sitting there still dressed in the same clothing he had gone out with the night before. He looked as though he had seen a ghost; he was spaced out, his mind a million miles away.

"Anton, what's wrong with you?"

"I did it again, Mom. I want to stop, but I did it again."

"This is a choice that you've made, and now you have to make a choice to stop it."

"Mom, if I don't get a handle on this now I will go crazy. I don't even like her; she is obnoxious and uncaring, full of vanity. What is wrong with me?"

I could tell that he was not really trying to insult the young lady; rather he was trying to come to terms with his own failures; his inability to exercise control. I had to help him. I understood how this could make him become and that he soon could lose all respect for women.

"We said we were going to find help but was so preoccupied with everything else around here. I'm sorry, I neglected you; but I will work on it first thing in the week, okay?"

"Okay," he agreed.

I left him sitting on the porch and went indoors. Sonja and her decorating crew were hard at work. I had to pull her away though – she had to see the gifts. She came upstairs with me.

"Look at these!" I opened the packages and she was blown away by the beauty of the gown.

"You went shopping without me, Mel?"

"Girl, don't you see gift paper? And didn't you tell Harold the sizes?"

She gasped for breath as she realised that Harold had given me the gifts.

"My word, that man is totally smitten."

"I'll say, everything here must have cost at least ten thousand dollars."

"Girlfriend, the jewelry alone is ten thousand dollars."

"Is it real?'

"Are you kidding me, Mel! Look at the certificate of authenticity?"

I could not believe it; I had assumed that it was high quality costume jewelry.

"What will he give you for Christmas, I wonder?"

"Sonja, I cannot accept these gifts."

"Don't start, Mel, be sensible. He is the owner of a successful restaurant. He is shopping within his means. You are not two teenagers; this relationship will be different – you are adults."

"Well, I guess so but ...." I sat on the bed; Sonja sat next to me.

"We kissed last Sunday. This time it was different. I asked him – I wanted him to kiss me. We talked about sex too, mutually deciding that we won't indulge in sin but ... what if he is really looking for more?"

"Sweetheart, he could buy you a Mercedes Benz. If he approaches you for sex and you say no – and I know you will say no - it is no! You do not have to repay him with sex, ever. Don't think about that at all. Just enjoy yourself, but be faithful to God, okay?"

I agreed with Sonja. She went back to the decorating and I proceeded to hang up the clothing. Then I noticed an envelope in the bag; I had not seen it before. My name was on the outside. It was a birthday card, one that you buy and write the words in yourself. It read ...

My love for you is like an ocean
That protects the sea bed and all life therein
Rivers run into the sea, but the sea flows nowhere
It is where it is, and there it will stay
Through hurricanes and thunderstorms
Winter's snow and summer's sun
And just like God has set the waters in its place
My heart is set on you, Mel, and by God's grace
I will stand with you through thick and thin
I will carry you as I soar on eagle's wings
And I will love you without reasoning
Unconditionally and with complete understanding
Because to me you are like a precious pearl
Uncut diamonds and pure rare gold
God bless you on this special day
Love, Harold

Tears of joy filled my eyes; I knew he loved me, but this was an eye-opener. *He loved me*! I called him - I had to. He answered as though he was expecting my call.

"I only just noticed your card."

"Sorry I missed your expression. I busted my brains on that poem."

He made me smile. "I love it. Do you really mean it?"

"Every word, Melinda."

"Thank you for loving me, Harold. I only hope that I can live up to your expectations."

"I am only expecting you to be yourself."

"I love you, too. I'll talk to you again later."

I finished up what I was doing and joined in the

work downstairs. We rearranged the house a little to allow for dancing. The party was due to start at 8:00 p.m., so we were not serving dinner but hors d'oeurves and cocktails. André and Harold decided what the music would be and left me out of it completely.

The next day we went to church early in the morning; we had lunch together then spent the afternoon quietly. No one said anything much to me at all. It was my birthday and all I got were very casual happy birthdays and hugs and kisses. Later will be greater I told myself.

The boys were washing the cars and cleaning up the yard before the party but Sonja and I went upstairs to chat. She was not going to be here much longer and we spent as much time as we could together. She was so instrumental in helping me to understand the Bible. I treasured this fine woman and had a wonderful plan to honour her at the party. I kept it a secret so no one knew what I had in mind.

I stayed in my room; I could not sleep and so decided to read the book I had bought from Apostle Duncan. André and Aphelia came up to my room around five o'clock; Aphelia was concerned about her mother and wanted to talk to me.

"Aunt Mel, I think that my mom will be very lonely when she gets back. I won't be there and she does not have any friends as close as you are to her. I am a bit concerned because she will return with all the beautiful memories of this past month; André and I now married and you and Harold are finding love. I don't know if she should go at all."

"Sonja is a strong woman," I reminded her.

"I know that but she is very reserved. She is only this

189

way around you. Otherwise she really goes nowhere and does nothing."

"Really?"

"Yes. I told her she should transfer, come back to Trinidad."

"Or … do you think I should go to New York with her for a while?"

They looked at each other, thinking that that was probably a good idea.

"That may be a good thing, Aunt Mel."

"Well, I'll let you in on my secret. I am going to surprise her tonight with the news that I am going to New York with her. I decided to go for a holiday – I'm spending two weeks."

Aphelia jumped up and hugged me, obviously thinking that it was a fantastic idea. I was concerned about leaving Anderson and so I asked André to keep an eye on him while I was away. I had to wait until the party to see if Sonja would have agreed to all of it. But if I know her as well as I think I do, she will be thrilled at the thought of my going to New York.

Harold arrived and for the first time he came upstairs. They really did not want me downstairs at all. I wondered what were they doing down there. However, I wanted to tell him about the plan instead of letting him find out with everyone else. I did not think I needed his permission but I thought it respectful to inform him first. He sat on the chair by the window enjoying the view of the backyard - the Poinciana tree really brightened up the garden. The mind is truly a marvel: in two seconds I imagined him being my husband, waking on mornings and sitting on this very chair in his bath robe, sipping coffee and looking out the window. Earth to Melinda!

"Harold, I'm going to New York on Tuesday."

"Just like that?"

"It is a surprise gift for Sonja and I was going to tell everyone tonight but then it dawned on me that I should tell you before making the announcement."

"How long will you be gone?

"Two weeks."

"You sounded like you were going for two years."

"No, no, just a short holiday."

"I honestly cannot object to that. I'll miss you though."

He got up from the chair and held my hands as he lodged a soft passionate kiss on my cheek.

"I guess you really do love me, huh. Happy Birthday, Mel" I still laugh at myself when I think how I blush and behave like a teenager whenever Harold acts a little romantic. My heart would beat faster and I think I actually shake a little. If, as they say, love is a disease, I had definitely caught it, and I didn't want to be cured.

Our guests started arriving a little after eight o'clock and all were there by 8:15. Sonja kept me upstairs because I did not know the exact agenda. We had invited a few friends, including Keith who had come with his girlfriend. Aphelia's entire wedding party was invited along with some of Sonja's family members. We even invited the neighbours on the corner; they were the only ones in the neighbourhood who really talked to us anyway; besides, this was not the forum to make friends.

As I started down the staircase I heard my sons singing. When did they practice? They did a lovely rearrangement of the well-liked, well-known and well-used, "Happy Birthday to You" but it was sounding like a brand new composition. Stepping down the winding staircase I could not see everything at the same time but in bits and pieces until I came to the bottom where Harold was waiting for me. I looked special but he felt it because I did wear the gown and accessories that he had bought me. He stretched out his hand and I took it. He then escorted me in fine style and sat me at the centre of attention. I was fifty but I felt like fifteen. Life had just started over for me and I was loving every moment of it.

My sons were back in my life in a more meaningful way than before; Sonja and I spent time together in person and not on the phone, having managed a telephone friendship for ten years; Harold, a man who had loved me since we met at a restaurant in town and sang our first song together in a Karaoke competition, was now my significant other, and Jesus had become my Saviour, personally. I really could not ask for anything more; I was contented with my life and found out that it really was a great life.

It seemed like everyone else felt the same as I did because I did not recognise my own house. I sat in wonderment at how lovely the guests looked, and the decorations! While I had rested in bed they had put up the finishing touches - I was pleasantly surprised. There were golden angels standing in strategic positions around the house, definitely representative of God's divine protection on our family, though they were just for the party. I thought that I would keep them there, but as quickly as the thought entered it vanished and I decided not to as they could become idols in my home and I did not want that. André had already showed me all of the figurines in the house that he thought I should get rid of and we did, so I knew he would probably say the same about these angels.

The applause was coming to an end and I thanked everyone for their love and for sharing this moment with me. Sonja paid tribute, the boys paid tribute and then it was Harold's turn to do so and he did it in song. How could I be so fortunate to have so many singers in my life? Harold sang Celine Dion's "My heart will go on"; it was amazing – I think everyone was crying. I almost didn't want to give Sonja her surprise gift anymore but I then thought it might be best if I did go. Here I was crazy in love and my thoughts about my relationship with Harold were getting dangerous – I needed to go to New York. It felt good to be human again though; at least I knew that I could feel something for someone again.

It was then Sonja's turn for a surprise honouring. I switched places with her; she was clueless as to what was going on. I made my speech telling our entire story to everyone and then I dropped the bombshell; she screamed in delight at the thought of our being in New York together for two weeks. But I think that her scream was really focused on the fact that I did get a Visa and Passport. I had flown on a plane once in my life, to Tobago, and had never left this nation to go anywhere else. So actually everyone in the family thought that I was deserving of that trip. Happy birthday to me!

Harold and I danced for a while, closing ourselves off to everyone else. I was scheduled to leave in two days. He was selfish that night but who could blame him. We left the guests and went into the backyard for a walk. Over the years I had developed the backyard to the point where we had our own little Botanical Gardens behind there. Dusk to dawn lights lit the round edged terrazzo-styled concrete slab walkway that was completely surrounded by a luscious green lawn. The fencing was covered with a variety of croton plants trimmed to about seven feet tall creating a private atmosphere; the rich colour of the leaves illuminated with the lights that lined the walls. I spent many days in this garden just to get away from the house and George's curses – it was like another world behind here. Harold held my hands and we walked through the garden, and then sat on the bench near the Poinciana tree.

"I am going to miss you, Melinda."

"I know; me too. We've seen so much of each other this month, I feel like we've been together for years."

"I want you to enjoy yourself in New York. I'll check on the boys for you."

"Thanks."

"These two weeks will feel like a lifetime. But I'll manage."

We chatted for a while longer then André came to say that some of the guests were ready to say goodbye. We went back in. The party was swinging. Everyone seemed to be having a good time. This was the last dance – Harold and André chose to play a song that I had recently learned to appreciate: "With Long Life You Will Satisfy Me." This song paid tribute to God's keeping power. It had a captivating beat and we all took to the dance floor. They played it a few times more as we bade farewell to our guests.

We sat in the living room exhausted but overjoyed that we had made the effort. We all chipped in to cleanup as we made conversation with each other, while reminiscing on the delightful evening and promising once again to stick together no matter what. Anderson said he needed to go to bed; he still could not put too much pressure on himself as his ribs were still not totally healed yet. Then something strange happened; we said nothing but it brought tears to my eyes, however. He turned to Harold and asked if he would accompany him upstairs, he wanted to talk to him. I was unsure if he had made a mistake or if he did it deliberately but he called Harold, 'Dad'. Without hesitation Harold obliged and spent about fifteen minutes upstairs. He said nothing when he returned and we did not ask any questions.

Harold left my house pretty late. We planned to have another family night on Monday and he promised to take us to the airport on Tuesday. We worked steadily until we had completely cleaned up after the party, then we all went to bed, full of very pleasant memories.

Chapter Eleven

wo weeks in New York turned into seven weeks and counting, and I was having a great time with Sonja. Aphelia was correct about Sonja's loneliness; she was doing well but the thought of being alone began to affect her and she was grateful to me for staying. We discussed her moving back to Trinidad but she had a project that she was working on and wanted to see it through. She did, however, intend to return to Trinidad some other time – in about a year or so.

My stay in New York eventually started to affect my relationship with Harold. We spoke to each other daily but Harold was not too pleased that I had stayed that long. He had a party planned at the restaurant for his birthday on August 22nd, but when I did not show he became even more upset. He told me how he felt in a casual manner but I did not take him seriously. I honestly did not pay attention to what the separation was doing to us being more concerned about Sonja. I could hear the edginess in his voice as we spoke one day. His short answers to my questions were quite noticeable.

"Alright Harold, what's going on?" I could take no more

of the strained conversation.

"Melinda, can you give me a date when you are actually coming back?"

I felt like he was crossing the line and that he should just let me be and so I replied with a hint of irritation and fury in my voice: "I don't know, but when I decide, I will let you know."

"That's not good enough."

"Excuse me!" I replied, feeling even more annoyed.

"I am not being unreasonable, Mel."

"Yes, you are."

"You told me two weeks; it's been almost two months."

"I am my own woman, Harold."

"Really? I thought you were my woman!"

I felt badly now because that statement reminded me that we were in a relationship. I had agreed to this and maybe I really was not being fair to him at all. That was the first time that we had quarrelled like that. I was a little shocked but, how could I have even thought that we would never fight? I did not respond to his last comment but remained silent on the phone.

"Mel, I have to go. Call me if you still want me to be your man."

He hung up. I really did not plan on staying in New York much longer but that was really uncalled for. I should have just told him that. Instead, by my silence, I must have triggered a sense of insecurity in him. I had called him later in the evening but he did not answer. I left a message but he never returned my call. I was beginning to get rather upset, I could not believe he was treating me this way and I became very confused. I wanted this relationship as much as he did but he seemed to have cut me off. I felt hurt because I was hoping that he had understood my position. I felt like Sonja needed me and I wanted to exercise freedom and enjoy life a little. I pulled out the birthday card and as I read the words again, tears filled my eyes. How could he treat me like this? Is this the same man who wrote me this poem?

Friday night finally came. I had had the longest week; Sonja and I had planned to go to Radio City Music Hall. Tyler Perry's "Madea Goes to Jail" was on that weekend and we had tickets for the show. I was looking at the tickets and realised that something was off.

"What's the date today?" I asked.

"The 5th," replied Sonja removing the rollers from her hair so she could style it.

"These tickets are for the 6th."

The clerk must have given us the wrong date and so we decided to just stay at home and watch T.V. or something as the show was the following day. Sonja knew that I was hurting and she told me that although she loved me being there, she would prefer that I returned home. I was angry with Harold at that point. How could he refuse to call me back? So childish I thought; maybe I should just stay in New York and discontinue the relationship. I had no intentions of putting up with a child at all. All my children were grown.

"Still no word from Harold yet?" I shook my head in the negative.

"Why don't you call him again?"

"You crazy or something? He owes me a call."

"Mel, you need to swallow your pride and call him back."

"I hope he's not holding his breath."

"You are so stubborn," she continued. "What have you decided, anyway?"

"Nothing yet."

"Melinda, wrong plus wrong will not amount to right. Harold is a fantastic complement to your life. You will be making a mistake if you give up on him now."

"A whole week, Sonja, and he hasn't called me back."

"I know, but, you should go home. I love you and I am so glad that you are here with me but you need to go home. You can come back again, but for now ... go home and fix things."

I knew that I had to go home but I did not like that I was being told to do so. Honestly I was thinking that Harold really should not dictate to me what I should or should not do. But was he really dictating my pace or did he just want me in his life so badly that he only expressed concern; distance does put a strain on relationships. I did plan to go back soon, not just for Harold but for Anderson and the others, though all reports were good. I was just mad at the way in which he seemed to be pushing me.

The doorbell rang. Sonja looked through the peep hole then spun around as though she had seen a ghost.

"Mel, it's Harold," she whispered.

"Harold?" I repeated, "You have to be joking."

"No, I'm not. Harold is here!" the doorbell rang again.

"I am letting him in."

"Of course, let him in."

Harold entered and greeted Sonja. Placing a small travel bag on the floor, he apologised to her for showing up unannounced and then fixed his eyes on me. It was no use asking him why he came because we all knew why he was there. Some part of me found that to be the single most identifiable act of his love for me, but I could also interpret it as an attempt to control. I really didn't think so though. This man was hurt; I felt sorry because he looked at me like a pitiful pup that was not given the bone he longed for. He did not even greet me. He just wanted to get things off his chest.

"Sonja, would you mind if I talked to Melinda alone for a moment?"

"Sure," she said and went to her room. I was still not too happy that he had just shown up like this and felt that he really should have called.

"Why didn't you call first?" He ignored my question and began his own dialogue.

"Melinda, if you are breaking up with me, the least you can do is tell me."

"What are you talking about?"

"I poured my life into this relationship; you give me two days notice that you are leaving then misled me saying that you were staying two weeks. It's been two months! How can you not expect me to be upset? I feel like you lied to me."

"I did not lie to you and furthermore I will not be controlled by anyone!"

My voice got a little louder and we began to argue, not hearing a word that we said to each other. Sonja was not at all happy about this and came outside.

"Harold, I cannot have this."

"Sonja, I'm sorry, but you were there, and privy to what we've experienced. Aren't you going to support me on this one?"

"Oh, I support you 100%, but I am still going to step in if you raise your voice at her in my presence and in my house."

"Ladies, I'm sorry. I better go – you're right – I should not have come, at least not in this state of mind."

By that time I was crying because my fairy tale relationship was looking like a nightmare. Sonja was the only one thinking straight at this point and gave us some good advice.

"Goodnight," said Harold and he turned to leave.

"Harold wait," Sonja interjected. "It's late and you two need to calm down. Where are you staying?"

"I have not even thought about that. I came directly from the airport."

"Okay, here's the deal: Come with me; you can use the guest room tonight. Let me show it to you. Tomorrow when your minds are in the right place, you two will discuss this."

My eyes followed them as they dissappeared into the guestroom. I could not help but wonder what in

God's name was going to happen to us. I was so unforgiving and did not even give him a chance to explain anything. I could hear them talking and just had to thank God again for a friend like Sonja.

"Let me tell you something, Harold, there is no way that you are going to lose Melinda, not now, not ever."

"Sonja, I feel like I've already lost her. I had so much confidence at first but now I feel defeated. I know I am not wrong about our feelings for each other. Am I?"

"You are not wrong. Trust me on this one, she is yours. Just before you rang the bell, we were talking about her returning home."

"Is she going home soon?"

"I don't know when she's going exactly, but…"

"See, she's been doing that for weeks. I don't know what to do. Thanks for standing with me anyway. Maybe I just love her too much."

I did not want to hear anymore; I knew he was hurting but he had to take responsibility for this. He should have returned my call instead of just showing up here. I went to the room I occupied at Sonja's -Aphelia's room really. I had learned a lot while in New York from going to church and Bible study with Sonja and I knew that this called for serious prayer. I knelt at my bedside and prayed asking God for guidance and humility. It is so comforting to know that God is concerned about everything that concerns us. When His Word says 'occupy till He comes' it means that we have a life to live. He cares about that life. If my life included Harold, I had better know how to talk to God about it. I felt comfortable talking to God about everything and casting all my burdens on Him.

The next morning I was up first. Sonja usually slept late on Saturdays; almost all New Yorkers who do not work on Saturdays sleep late on that day. I don't get it. Well it's not like I can see anything but concrete through these windows anyway. I made Harold breakfast and decided to serve it to him in bed. That was my way of apologising. I knocked on the door ...

"Come in."

"Good morning, I made you "breakfast in bed" but, you are up already so I guess it is just breakfast in the bedroom."

"Good morning, Mel," he said, with a faint smile on his lips.

I was happy that I had made him smile. I turned to leave and said, "Enjoy your breakfast."

"You really think I could eat?"

He said that like he would fast until we made up. I turned around and just looked at him. He stared back at me. We behave so foolishly at times, it is unbelievable. Here we were both infatuated with each other yet neither of us wanted to be the first to apologise. Harold is a gentleman though and I, well I needed deliverance from my attitude.

"Mel, we need to talk about this. Can I please have a word with you?"

"I'm listening."

"I'm sorry for raising my voice and for embarrassing you. I just feel like our relationship is over and I don't understand why."

"I'm sorry, too, but you are way too insecure."

"Insecure? You are unreasonable. I think we have something extra special and if so I want to preserve it. All I want is for you to be in Trinidad so I can date you."

"I have absolutely no intentions of giving up on you or our relationship."

"But how are we going to be in a relationship if you are thousands of miles away?"

"It's only for a short period."

"Two months is not short, Mel, at least not for me; and you still cannot give me the date that you are coming back. If you don't know when, how I am supposed to know what the real deal is. We need to get to know each other before ...." He did not finish the sentence.

"Before what?"

Harold sighed deeply, thinking carefully about what he was going to say.

"Like I told you previously, I am not in this just for the sake of being in it. I'm in because I would like to make you my wife one day. I know we've not been dating that long but if I'd thought for one minute that you were not the one, I would not have taken it this far."

Is he blind? I thought. Can he not see that he is the one who withdrew and left a void?

"The last thing you said to me was that I should call if I still wanted to be with you right?"

"Right!" he confirmed, obviously remembering our last conversation.

"I did, and you did not pick up your phone. I called again, same thing; so I left a message and you never called back. I am not prepared to ..."

"Hold on, what message? And here's my phone, check the recently dialed calls list; there must be at least a hundred calls and all of them are to your number. You shut your phone off and that's why I took an airplane out here. I even tried calling you from the airport."

"I didn't turn off my phone!" I protested, although he had me thinking that I was going crazy.

I took his phone to check because that was strange. All the dialed calls did have my name. I was even more confused so I checked the actual number he was dialing.

"Harold! This is not my number!"

"What do you mean it is not your number?"

"The last digit of my number is '9' not '6'; you were not calling me."

"Oh Lord, no!"

The expression on his face was indescribable; a mixture of relief and bewilderment, in addition to sheer joy at the thought that he definitely was not losing me at all.

"Melinda," he began to confess, "shortly after we spoke that day my cell phone died. Well, let me tell the truth. I was angry and threw the cell phone aside and it fell and broke."

"You destroyed the phone in anger?"

"I did not deliberately destroy it. I put it down on the banister on the porch and it fell - but I did not put it down too easily."

"Next time you confess, please tell the whole truth. You were mad and mashed up the phone!"

"Okay I was mad – madly in love with you." He was too cute; my anger began subsiding rapidly. "However, your number and a few others were saved to the phone and not the sim card so I just dialed the number and saved it with your name on this new phone. I never looked at the number again - only the name. I did not realise that I had punched in a wrong number."

"I wonder what happened to the message I sent you."

He walked towards me and I could no longer see the lines on his forehead since they had disappeared as he was now relaxed.

"I'm glad that I did not get the message, because if I did I would not have made this trip. I'd almost forgotten how beautiful you are. I love you dearly - and I miss you like crazy."

Harold hugged me and that hug said a lot more than we had said to each other in weeks. We laughed at ourselves, realising that this mix-up had really been caused by a simple mistake. Isn't it sad how so many disastrous outcomes can occur because of a petty mistake? It is so important to "be slow to anger". Harold and I could have taken this to a level of hurt that could have well destroyed our relationship if we had not calmed down and talked it over amicably. We apologised to each other and forgave one another. We each took responsibility for what had happened.

I was so grateful that we did, I really loved this man and was a little anxious to see what the future held for us. Oops! Philippians 4:6, "Be careful (anxious) for nothing, but in everything by prayer and supplication, with thanksgiving, let your requests be made known to

God." These were my watchwords where my relationship with Harold was concerned.

We chatted a while longer. He explained his behaviour and although I did not fully accept his position, I understood his point. I understood that we would not agree on everything but must compromise in order to live in harmony. Harold stated that he is not prepared to carry on a long distance relationship at all. He mentioned Evelyn, and I had to listen to what he was not saying.

"Wait a minute, don't you trust me?"

"Of course, I trust you."

"No, you don't. Why are you comparing me with Evelyn?

"I did that?"

"Yes, you did. My staying here this long is completely different to Evelyn leaving her husband in Grenada and deceiving you."

"Mel, I did not say that it was the same."

"You didn't have to. I will give you the very same advice you gave to me. I am not Evelyn."

"I know that, honey."

"Then act like you know that. This probably reminded you of the pain that you went through losing her, but Lord no, I'm not her. All of this insecurity you've shown by coming to New York is indicative of the fact that you are still skeptical about women. Be careful not to put me in that category."

"I hear you, I'm sorry. I guess we are all prisoners for real."

I promised him that I would come home in a week and he took the next available flight back to Trinidad. I made myself a pledge that I would be careful not to spoil my relationship with Harold, although I was firm on how I felt when he "tracked me down". I really should commit from now. It is foolish to think that I can fully commit only after the wedding ceremony. We should be dating exclusively or else there won't even be a wedding. It was really unfair in the first place to treat Harold that way. If something happened and I had to stay that would be different but staying just because I felt like it, with no explanations nor reasons, maybe I was in fact being unreasonable.

My last days in New York with Sonja flew by quickly; we made sure to have a time and a half. We did go to see Tyler's play on Broadway, among other things, and I shopped for everyone in the family.

I kept my promise to Harold and returned home the following week.

Chapter Twelve

veryone was happy that I was home again, especially Harold. He was like a little spoilt child. A holiday was really what I needed though. Anthony and Anton had gone back to their apartments; Andy did not go job searching but stayed at home and was faithful to his therapy sessions with Dr. Matthews. Aphelia was a great help, cooking daily for her husband and brother-in-law and keeping the house for me in my absence even though she had her own apartment to see about. Harold checked on them from time to time and even had Anderson work with him at the restaurant now and again just to get him out of the house.

Keith had done the most wonderful thing for Andy and we were very appreciative. He spoke to the Manager of the company on his behalf. Withholding certain details about the real problem, he told him that Andy had been under a lot of pressure and was in therapy but he was recovering nicely. The Manager, thankfully, was understanding because Andy had been an excellent worker and apparently his absence had left a void in the department. He decided that if Andy did solve his problems and wanted to return to work he would do everything in his power to rehire him. True to his promise, he interviewed him and Andy was rehired. Saving up five months of vacation leave paid off because they did the necessary paperwork and documented his absence as approved vacation. In a week's time he was due back on the job. Talk about favour from God; everyone deserves a second chance and Andy got his. In a way I was glad that I had left him to get better on his own. I know that André kept a close eye but he had to want to get better for himself as well. I believed God for the deliverance of my entire family. I must say I am beginning to appreciate the Psalmist David's passion for God. Awesome is HE! I thought that André was crazy but now that I have experienced God for myself, I am completely sold out.

Harold continued to build his business and always looked for different ways to satisfy the needs of his patrons. The story of the establishment of "Le Paradis Magique" was intriguing; he actually started the business catering to the social needs of God-fearing people who did not want to hang out in places with undesirable music and illicit activities. He felt that a good business idea was to provide an alternative. Although he played some choice secular music, the repertoire was primarily gospel – of all genres. I had no clue that there was so much gospel music out there.

One of Harold's ideas was to hook up with producers who visited once per month at his invitation. He wanted to attract young people to the restaurant, and also to expose singers to the world of entertainment. So he birthed "Talent Search" which showcased on the last Friday of every month. It was open to everyone. They brought their music and sang live so that their talent could be recognized. This was instrumental in increasing the amount of local gospel music available on the market. It also gave some talented people a career break. This is how André came to produce a single. He occasionally sang at the restaurant but also took part in "Talent Search."

The months rolled on and life returned to normalcy for my family. Anthony and Anton visited quite often on weekends and would go to church with us whenever they came. Harold and I got engaged in October of that year, but did not have a wedding date at the time. I knew by then I was ready for marriage. Emotionally my relationship with George had completely faded into nothingness so the fact that he had died less than a year ago was not relevant to me at all. I thought that I had recovered quite well; I felt good in my body and my emotions were intact for the most part.

However, I was a bit concerned about my sexuality and even more concerned as to what would happen when the time came for me to be intimate with Harold. We did kiss once in a while, never prolonged the event and of course there was nothing beyond that. I did wonder though whether I was closed off or if it was a choice I had made because of my commitment to Christ. The difference was difficult for me to recognize at that point. I spoke to Harold about it and told him that I wanted to get some counseling before we set a wedding date. He agreed, of course, and so we had two separate counseling sessions with Pastor Joseph and his wife, Monica. I had my personal sessions and we had marriage counseling sessions together. I did wonder if marriage counseling was necessary at our age but at each session we learned something new and longed to go back to the subsequent sessions.

Pastor Joseph decided that he would let his wife, Monica, counsel me on my personal concerns and she encouraged me to ensure that I had forgiven George totally and completely. I learned that the inability to forgive produced a seed and my heart was like an incubator; it provided the atmosphere for the seed to germinate and it would inevitably grow in me. Not in

George - but in me. Holding on to George's abusive acts against me could only hurt me at this point but not George. In the long run Harold would be hurt; but George was nowhere in the picture and could not be hurt; even if George were alive I would still only hurt myself. I thought about this over and over again and the more I did the more I released myself to forgive on a daily basis. I prayed that God would give me the grace to forgive completely. I knew for certain that I would one day want the sexual aspect of my life to be operational in all its grandeur, especially when I thought of the fact that Harold would be asking me for a wedding date soon. I made up my mind to forgive so that I could heal internally. Inner peace was my goal.

Christmas was approaching and Anthony and Anton decided to come home for Christmas as we had not had a Christmas together for a very long time. I invited Sonja to come home as well but she declined; she said that she could only come for one event and she preferred to come for my wedding which was finally planned for Easter Monday. We all spent a wonderful Christmas together and rang in the New Year with a simple after-church party at home.

I had another opportunity to be with all the boys again and was eternally grateful to them for indulging me although they were all grown men. They continued to pursue their individual goals and dreams; not that everything was silky smooth with no problems; life will always have its challenges, but we must learn how to deal with them. I was however proud to see the progress that each of them had made; Anton had been going to therapy for his addiction and had a steady girlfriend named Joanne. Sleeping around was not an option once he had decided to date her exclusively. Joanne was very intelligent but something just did not sit right with her and me at all. I stayed out of their way though, determined he must make his own choices.

Anderson still remained at home with me and was committed to his job once more. He buried himself in a back log of work from the office and brought home a few boxes of clients' files to work on. This kept him busy but he did go out a few times with Keith and their circle of friends. His visits with Dr. Matthews were twice a month at that point.

André and Aphelia also had some great things going on for them as well: she was pregnant, the baby due in July of the following year. Anthony, however, was still very reserved and withdrawn; he would step out a little to have fun with us but go right back into his shell afterwards. I was beginning to get very concerned about him so I decided to have a heart-to-heart talk with him after the New Year's Day celebrations. I knocked on his door that afternoon and he invited me in. He was reading the newspapers when I went in. I did not know how I would approach the subject and so found something else to start talking about.

"The crime rate is extremely high. I wonder what we need to do to bring it down," I said reading the headlines of the newspapers. He then pulled the papers from in front of his face to his lap. He looked at me and I knew he saw right through me.

"Mom, you do not want to talk about crime, what's up?"

"Okay, how are you doing Anthony?"

"Fine, I guess. What's on your mind?"

"You!" I said without going around in circles anymore.

"Me, what for?"

"Anthony you are so withdrawn and I am worried."

215

"Mom, I just like to be quiet."

"It's more than that, Anthony. You are always by yourself. Are you dating anyone?"

"No, but what's wrong with that?"

He did not even see a problem and I was wondering if I should just leave it alone.

"Nothing is wrong with it. I am just trying to find out how you're going."

"Mother, you do not need to be concerned about me. I like being quiet and only speak when I need to."

He was being truthful because I saw him stand up to Gerard when we first met him and then he joined with his brothers to beat the crap out of him when we rescued Andy. He had spoken up on numerous occasions concerning other things as well. So maybe he was right and I didn't need to be worried at all.

"Well, I just never see you any other way that's all."

"You know what? I have to go to the Hyatt on Tuesday to make a presentation on behalf of the company; why don't you come along so you can see me in action? It would be fun to have my mother with me. My colleagues will love that."

"You are saying two things; you want me there or not?"

"Yes, I'm joking. Please come I will pick you up at 8:30."

I thought: 'Wow' this will be a first; so I decided that I would definitely go. Tuesday arrived so fast. Anthony was a completely different person that day. He was dressed in a business suit and spoke with such competence and charisma that I simply did not know who this man was. I needed to see him in action, among his colleagues, just doing his thing. It took all my concerns away and I prayed, thinking that speaker, my son, would one day be speaking from a pulpit for the honour and glory of God.

Once again the house was half empty as Anthony and Anton went back to their lives. My relationship with God grew and I took official membership with the church. All was well and I could not have asked for anything more. Or so I thought...

A couple weeks after New Year's, I returned home from a lunch date with Harold and I saw Andy's car parked outside. I wondered how come he was home so early. André had the day off and he and Aphelia had gone shopping for baby accessories. Harold came in with me and we called out to Andy but he did not answer; we just thought he was taking a nap or something. I often helped Harold with some of the paper work for the business when there is a backlog. His secretary gets overwhelmed sometimes. He was checking them over with me before he took it back to his office.

"You need to hire an assistant secretary, Harold."

"Why should I when I have an excuse to see you more often."

"Mr. Cave, I will send you a bill."

'Then I will just have another excuse to come over here – to pay my bill."

We laughed; we had become extraordinarily comfortable around each other and were very open and honest. We had a few arguments but tried to work out our differences with the least amount of heartache possible. Sometimes the arguments were about

Anderson; Harold felt like I still held on to him and would not let him go. I almost lost him once; he showed vulnerability to abuse, how could I not keep him close? I thought however I overdid it when I cancelled a date with Harold to stay at home because André went out with Aphelia and Andy was home alone.

"I don't believe you, Melinda," Harold complained. I remembered the argument vividly. "Anderson is twenty-eight years old!"

"So why can't we just order food and stay here tonight?"

"It's not about that; we do stay here sometimes."

"Then what is it about?"

"How can you cancel a date with me because Andy is home alone? That is so absurd."

"Stop arguing with me, Harold. You know you can't win."

"Fine, I am going home. I'll eat alone."

"You're acting like a child."

"Maybe because I want you to treat me like one sometimes. Like Anderson."

I did not believe that he was serious until I heard the car start and he really did leave. I was stubborn as usual and did not call him till the following day. He has since given up on arguing with me where Andy was concerned.

We were almost finished with the paperwork when André and Aphelia came home; she was feeling ill and had to go straight to her room. André asked us to pray for her - she was vomiting profusely. It started happening a few minutes after she had eaten fried chicken and chips for lunch. He had to make a few stops on the way here so she could throw up. I told him he should have taken her to the hospital, but she did not want to go. We laid hands on her and prayed but I warned her that if the vomiting did not cease within a reasonable time-frame, we must take her to to the hospital. She fell asleep a short while afterwards and so we just let her be.

André was bringing in the packages from the car when he too commented on the fact that Anderson was home so soon. He asked us about it and we told him that he was probably sleeping because he did not answer when we called. That was actually the beginning of an event in my life that I did not see coming at all. Harold went back to his office, Aphelia slept for a couple hours and André and I chatted about all kinds of stuff in the kitchen. We used to spend a lot of time together when George was ill so I was happy that he still found time to spend with me though he was now a married man. Around 4:00 p.m. I decided to go to Andy's room, just to check on him. The door was closed and I knocked - no answer. I called out to him and still he did not respond. I tried the door handle and although it was closed it was not locked and so I opened it to see if he was in there at all. He was; he lay on his bed covered from the neck down.

"Andy," I called, "are you feeling sick or something?"

There was no answer. I went to the bed to shake him so I could find out what was going on with him. I reached out and touched his shoulder; he felt as cold as ice and somewhat stiff. I ignored the reality for a moment. He lay on his side, his face to the wall, I could not see his face; I tried to turn him over but there was no life. I could no longer ignore the truth - he was dead.

I held on to him and screamed so loudly my voice echoed through the house. André sped up the stairs to see what had happened and had to pry my hands off my dead son. I had to be dreaming. I could not believe that Anderson was dead. Aphelia heard the noise and came over to the main house. André could not move because of how he had to hold on to me. When he heard her voice he shouted to her not to come upstairs but to call the police immediately because it seemed like Anderson had committed suicide.

He eventually got me out of the room and in the corridor. Aphelia started up the stairs again but he begged her to stay downstairs since she had been vomiting earlier on and he could not risk her getting more upset. André got me into my room which was just a few doors down and put me to sit down. I was fighting him all the way and he had a difficult time trying to keep me back from grabbing on to Anderson. He used the phone in my room to call Harold and told him he needed to come immediately. He then called Anthony and Anton. He was crying as he spoke to them but still tried his best to keep me from running back to Anderson's room.

The police came about fifteen minutes later and checked out the scene. What they found was the story of a man who had lost all hope. They found an empty pill bottle, suicide notes and HIV test results from the hospital on his night stand. Anderson had taken the entire bottle of sleeping pills – then went to sleep – and never woke up. He left a note for each member of his family and one for Keith. He had been tested for HIV in June last year when he was in the hospital; the results then were negative. It is customary to test every six months if you feel you've been exposed; so when the hospital sent a reminder, he went for another test. This time the results were positive - Andy immediately thought he could not handle it and evidently felt that he did not want to live any more. He took his life and part of mine. I could not believe my eyes and ears and had a tough time coming to terms with the calamity. How could I have missed it? How could I not have known? Everyone tried to comfort me but I felt as though I should have sensed his pain. Many believed that the test results did it because he seemed to have been making progress over the past months. The notes also seemed to suggest that he had only decided on suicide after receiving the test results. The police gave everyone their notes to read. I could hardly see but I took mine. I wanted to understand why, how could he take his life?

My dear mother,

I cannot ask for you to be any better a mom, but you should have let me die at Gerard's hands. I refuse to live with AIDS, I refuse to put you through any more pain and I sure as hell would not let you care for another sick man in your life. I love you and I know that you are hurting as you read this but you will be better soon. Bye bye Mom

Love always, Anderson

Dear Dad (Harold),

I really do love you, you have replaced my father in my life, I wish you came into our lives earlier. Please take care of my mother.

Love, Anderson

I could only call on God now. He was the only person that could take this pain away. The undertakers carried Anderson's body to the Forensic Sciences Lab. I wept bitterly. All the other men in my life, my sons and Harold, could do nothing to comfort me. I just had to go through my pain and let time take care of it.

Anderson was buried three days later but I buried myself for another three weeks. I hardly spoke to anyone and did not leave the house at all. Harold came to see me every morning and also in the evening - I was not eating well, my eyes were dark and I did not comb my hair for days. He decided to bring a doctor to the house who prescribed tranquilizers but I refused medication. All I needed was Jesus and time; I knew that.

I would go into Andy's room every day, sit on the bed and cry like a baby. I spent most of my day in prayer, bombarding God's throne room with the question, why? Anthony and Anton stayed at the house until I began to act normal again. It took me a while but I just needed to talk myself through it. Everything was going so well, then this. Of course, God never gave me a reason why. I was careful not to blame Him though.

Slowly but surely I came out of mourning and began picking up where I had left off. I believe that this pain will never totally leave me but I will manage it. One evening I sat on the bench in the backyard looking at the poinciana tree. In this nation, we affectionately call it 'the flaming poinciana'; its beautiful exotic flowers red as fire seem to cover the entire plant when in full bloom. Her branches were spread wide across the yard touching the walls on the backside of the house. The boys damaged this tree when they were kids, leaving a gash on the trunk – that part of the tree never sent out any more branches and remained scarred; however, the tree had grown beautifully otherwise. I saw myself in that tree and saw Andy as the gash. In time I decided that I would move on, I would grow on - but I knew there would always be that gash to remind me of a part of me that had been torn away.

Chapter Thirteen

alentine's Day was swiftly approaching and Harold had a gala event planned at his restaurant. It was a month since Anderson's death and I was doing fine for the most part. I began to laugh again and went to church and meetings and did everything I used to - except one, the marriage counseling. Harold and I had not been to a session since Andy had died. During this period he was more like a big brother than a fiancé and it seemed like our relationship had changed. He wanted to discuss the matter with me but really did not even know how to approach the topic. A few days before Valentine's, he thought it best to just be straight. He called and asked if I wanted to go to dinner; honestly, it was only then I remembered that I had a fiancé. I became really apologetic but I still did not go out to dinner that night but instead, we ordered food and stayed home. After dinner Harold reminded me about the function.

"Mel, about my Valentine's Day party, I don't even know how to begin ..."

"We are supposed to do a duet." I had almost forgotten.

"Listen, if you are not up to it, I'll just do a solo."

I opted for his doing the solo because I was not sure if I could pull it off. That was the second thing I turned down that night and by that time Harold was beginning to show signs of concern.

"Sweetheart," he said as politely and as charmingly as ever, "I'm missing my fiancée; our relationship has certainly changed a bit over the past few weeks."

"I know it has, but there is no need to worry."

"I am not worried, just concerned."

He held my hands and was obviously trying very hard to communicate his dilemma without giving the impression that he did not care about the other aspects of my life.

"I want to say I love you without you thinking I mean, 'I love you with the love of God'".

I was totally confused by that remark at first but then I became conscious of the fact that we did not display any emotions other than brotherly love to each other since Andy passed.

'Oh my word,' I said to myself, 'Girl, you must be tranquilized'. I have always tried to let the dead be the dead and go on with the living, but this one got me really good; I guess if Andy had died by some other means it would have been different, easier even. But if someone decides that he no longer wants to live, those he leaves behind must wonder ... I still did not respond to Harold. My mind raced like a three year old thoroughbred on the racing track. Harold tightened his grip on my hands to get my attention.

"Melinda, we have not even been to counseling for a while either."

"I am not ready to resume just yet."

"That is what concerns me. I don't know what's happening to us. I want you back but at the same time I don't want to push you – I don't want to upset you – I am grieving for Andy too."

"I understand perfectly," I said, trying very hard to give the impression that I was on the same page with him. "Why don't you call and set up an appointment for next week?"

"Okay," he replied "but tell me, do you really want to go?"

"No," I said honestly.

"Mel, can I ask you another question?"

"Sure."

"Are we still getting married in April?"

"Do you want a wife who cannot get her mind off her dead son?"

"We will get through it – together."

"Harold, it's really hard for me right now."

"Is that a no?"

"It's an *I don't know.*"

I could not think about the wedding. I wanted to fall asleep for as long as possible and when I got up Anderson should be alive. Harold just sat back in the chair, took in a huge breath and blew through his mouth.

"You need to climb over this barricade. The rest of the

family needs you. I need you."

"Harold, can you give me a few more weeks? I am not able to function right now."

"Absolutely, take as much time as you need, but do not alienate me." He was beginning to sound as though he was begging me and I really did not like making him feel that way at all. I really did not know how to climb out of the pit and continue to pursue this wonderful new life. I knew however that I had to find solutions and fast, or else I would have created yet another prison.

"One more thing, Honey," Harold began as my mind came back to the issue at hand, "even if you don't feel like singing on Saturday, would you please come to the Valentine's Day function with me?"

I told him that I would go but I honestly did not feel like it at all. I had to will myself to go and I had only a few days to do it. Oh how I needed Sonja right now; she would be able to help me pull through. She was anointed for these tasks.

When Harold left for home that night I knew that all was not well with him; I knew he saw through me, but held back. I did the best I could at the time. I called Sonja. I needed someone to talk to about this. I told her everything about my conversation with Harold, and of course she too was concerned. She, however, told me that if I missed the function I would have to answer to her. She reminded me of all the great times that Harold and I shared. She said that this was my time now and though I hurt for Andy, I really should not give up my life but push through the pain and live again. Sonja really knew how to make me feel better when I was at my worst.

I did push myself. I did not even wait for Harold to

call Pastor Joseph but did so on my own to set up the appointment.

I attended the Valentine's Day function and was so glad I did. André sang one of his own compositions and I thought it was one for the charts; the patrons were truly moved. Although many couples could identify with the song, 'In Love a Second Time', I knew he sang it especially for Aphelia.

Harold was pretty busy making sure everything went smoothly but he made time to sit with me for a while. I had to ask him about the decor and the place settings. Wherever did he come up with the idea; it was so creative! The champagne glasses were a definite hit. Each couple was pre-registered and mandated to send in a picture. Harold then had the picture placed at the bottom of the glasses which were specially made and was to be used for a special toast. They could not see the picture until they drank. You can imagine the giggles, drinking from a glass then seeing yourself and the one you love inside of it – hilarious. The glasses were a token – theirs to take home with them. The centre pieces were bouquets of imitation red roses made from velvet. Pillars with greenery, adorned with decorative lights, were stationed at strategic points throughout the restaurant. Photographers were also on hand to capture the memories. The music was carefully selected and although it serenaded lovers, it gave Glory to God Almighty. This was the perfect place to be on Valentine's Day. Harold went all out with turning the restaurant into a romantic atmosphere – I am certain that the patrons felt like they truly got their money's worth.

Finally, Harold asked me to dance; I thought he never would. He looked great and I felt great. The man I loved is the one who made Valentine's special for so many couples. LeAnn Rimes' How *Do I Live Without You?* is a song I love. The words meant a lot to me and I suppose to Harold as well. Harold let the song talk for him this time – not that he was short on words – he just stared into my heart through my eyes hoping that I got the message. He leaned forward and kissed me. "I love you, Melinda. Please marry me." It was like another proposal. "Have you decided if the wedding is on yet?"

"It is on Harold. I want to marry you." He did not say another word but the way he held me said everything.

We went back to the table but before he ventured into the kitchen to ensure that everything was going well, he gave me a gift – one that I will treasure forever. A gold chain, 18" in length with a pendant. A golden locket about one inch in diameter with Anderson's face etched on the inside. That was such a wonderful idea. I looked at him and did not know what to say.

"I don't want you to forget about Anderson."

"Thank you," I said holding back the tears. "Do you remember that night, immediately after my party when he called you upstairs?

"Yes, I do."

"You never spoke about it. Why did he call you?"

"It was nothing really. The bruise to his ribs was hurting pretty badly that night and he wanted me to pray for him. I was wondering why he called me 'Dad', so I asked him. He said that the man that loved his mother he considers his father."

"I am really glad he accepted you, Harold. No wonder you two got along so well."

"I think that all your children have accepted me,

Melinda, and that is what makes this so much easier."

In the days following I paid special attention to spending quality time with Harold once again and pretty soon we were well on our way to planning our wedding and the honeymoon. I did leave a little space in my heart to grieve for Andy but kept it in a private chamber; only God and I were allowed in.

Sonja kept her promise and flew to Trinidad to stand with me as my maid of honour. Harold chose his brother to be his best man and his mother gave him away. Our wedding was simple, yet as fabulous an occasion as ever could be. The house came alive with excitement and we had a wonderful time.

The ceremony took place at home at 10 o'clock in the morning followed by a simple lunch. There were only about fifty people present. I felt like royalty: he sang to me and we danced. I believe at that point I totally released myself to love again. When it was time to stick the cake I wanted to decline but you know how weddings are - the guests simply cannot wait for moment. Approaching the table that was nicely decorated with fern leaves and red roses, I don't know how I kept it together; I was shaking in my shoes.

This is the most beautiful cake I have ever seen, I thought to myself. Four tiers; the bottom layer was probably twenty inches in diameter and each layer was a couple inches smaller than the previous. The icing pattern swirled all around the cake and small roses accentuated each curve. At the top was a bouquet of fresh flowers and not the traditional ceramic bride and groom figurine. For this occasion we chose the song, *I Will Love You Faithfully*. I was beginning to get incredibly nervous having to kiss him in front of everybody but I acted quite bravely. Although Harold and I had kissed before, this kiss was the longest and it was different. I knew then that I was delivered from the effects of the abuse. The counseling with Pastor Monica had worked and I was ready for more than a kiss I was certain. My mind wandered briefly on the goodness of God as I silently thanked Him for my deliverance.

The wedding reception was over just as the sun began to set in the western sky. Harold and I planned to spend the night at his house. Miami was the spot chosen for the honeymoon. The flight was early the following day.

As I entered his apartment, I could not believe what he had done with the place for our wedding night. He turned his home into a virtual garden with all types of fragrant flowers. There were also wines and champagne as well as light treats. He even prepared a CD with specially selected soft music. Where did he find the time to do all these things? It was clear that he had put a lot of thought into this event. After years of being raped, I thought that I would never give myself to another man. I broke out of that prison through prayer and forgiveness and was now like a new woman with Harold. I did get flashbacks but was able to dismiss any negative effects and yielded totally to my husband. I was truly having a 'Heaven on Earth' experience.

We enjoyed an almost picture perfect honeymoon and although I thought about Andy from time to time, I never let it depress me at all. I enjoyed feeling like a teenager in love with my Prince Charming. Harold made sure that I never stepped out of the clouds; he said that we would get real when we got back home. He spared nothing.

After two weeks of honeymooning, we returned home. We mutually agreed to live primarily at my house and would use Harold's as a getaway from time to time. I got a wonderful surprise on my return. Sonja and the boys had completely redecorated my bedroom. It was a wedding present. I was in awe stepping into a place that I did not know at all. I felt like we were just beginning our honeymoon – a lifelong honeymoon.

The first thing I noticed was the colour of the room. I had never used any other colour but off-white; it was now a light jade green with darker green accents. They chose green as it represented freshness and growth. They kept the bed but changed the mattresses and pillows and all the linens. The carpet, ceiling, lighting, drapes and bedroom door were also changed. The décor of the bathroom was even more unique. The tiles, walls and floor were totally redone; it now looked like a beach scene. I did not recognize my room but most of all, nothing there reminded me of George; that was Sonja's main goal.

Good friends are very hard to come by; I would not trade that woman for all the tea in China.

Chapter Fourteen

May 25th was the anniversary of George's death. In only one year I was able to find myself; I had got my life back. God had restored those things that I held dear to my heart but did not get the chance to live out with George. All the events of my life prior to George's death were playing like a movie in my head. It was midnight and I could not sleep. Harold had worked all day at the restaurant and was sound asleep next to me. I looked at him – the happiest man alive, I thought. We had been married for six weeks. Jesus had brought peace into our lives. Our commitment to God and each other produced waves of joy - a happy life. We truly made each other happy.

I had totally gotten over all the hurt and pain. I remembered everything but the memory of it hurt no more. I could think about it without feeling as though I needed deliverance. My past had groomed me and shaped me into who I had become. All I wanted to do now was to serve the Lord in spirit and in truth; to be loyal to my beloved husband, who had promised to be at my side through thick and thin, and to be a presence in the lives of my children and my grandchildren, the first grand was scheduled to arrive soon.

There was one thing I needed to do. Over the years Anderson had managed to save over a hundred and fifty thousand dollars; his insurance yielded another two hundred thousand and there were other cheques from investments that I got after he passed; the total amounted close to half a million dollars - quite an achievement for such a young man. As the Executor of Andy's will, I looked for something to do in his name and his memory; something that would help anyone in his position to pull through and not suffer the same fate as he had.

I got up and sat at the table next to the bedroom window, praying to God and asking His direction as to what I should do. At church the week before, Pastor Joseph had announced special plans and for some reason what he said came to mind. He wanted to expand the various community and ancillary ministries that visited prisons, hospitals, convalescent homes, adult care facilities and such like. As I prayed that day I felt strongly that I should join one of those ministries and also provide financial support for them. How? I wondered; then as clear as day I saw three mini buses parked in front of the church with the church's name printed on them. I could not recall our church owning any buses at all; then it dawned on me, I should donate the money to buy the buses. I felt my heart settle in satisfaction and I knew that that was my answer. I purposed to call Pastor Joseph when the office opened the following day to schedule an appointment. I continued to pray and seek God's face concerning a number of other things and felt a release in my spirit. I then went to bed and slept like a baby.

The next day when we got up it seemed as though Harold and I both had had a night of spiritual encounters and we started talking about our experiences. I told him what I wanted to do with

Anderson's money and he thought that it was a fantastic idea. He also had some ideas of his own and wanted to discuss them with me.

"I am not getting younger, Mel. I am ready to retire."

"Already!" I exclaimed, thinking that he was too young for that. "What about the restaurant?"

"André loves that place," he started. "I have not spoken to him yet but I am wondering if he would like to assume ownership."

"Ownership or management?" I asked seeking clarification.

"Ownership. I am beginning to feel the need to recruit someone else to carry it on."

Harold was only fifty-five years old but thought that the time had come for him to slow down.

"Well, that sounds good, but what about the ministry that I want to get involved in; wouldn't we be separated very often as I go out with the church?"

"We will, but this won't happen immediately you know; it will take a few years."

"Hmmm, it does sound like a plan. Have any idea how André will respond?" I asked, having never asked André anything about managing a restaurant.

"No clue," he replied. "We'll see, but he is my first choice."

Harold then went to do business at the bank and other errands and I went to see the Church's Secretary. Unexpectedly someone had cancelled an appointment so I was able to see Pastor Joseph immediately. I stepped into his office feeling rather confident about what I was supposed to do and just laid it out. Pastor sat back in his chair whispering praises to God at almost every sentence I spoke. When I was through he got up, walked to the filing cabinet and removed a file. He handed me the file. I was wondering what for, as I looked at the label which read 'Minutes'. He told me to open it and read the contents. The file contained a document: "Minutes of board meeting dated May 24th." The minutes were not even typed yet. At that meeting they decided that the church needed to raise funds to purchase three mini buses in order to transport members to the various institutions for ministry; and other things, of course. I stared in awe at the wonderful God we serve. I lifted my head from the document and smiled.

"I am going to the bank to have the draft made," I said, full of confidence and satisfaction in my spirit.

"Sister Melinda, go with God and may He continue to use you for His honour and glory."

'What a Mighty God we serve,' I thought as I left the office and drove to the bank. There is a portion of scripture that came to my mind, "And we know that all things work together for good to those who love God; to those who are the called according to His purpose." Romans 8:28. I just had to believe that my life was a big setup for all the good that God was now sharing with me. I remembered Joseph, who seemingly lost it all after being sold into slavery to some Egyptians but God had a plan and the very act that his brothers used to destroy him was the opening he needed to being tremendously used of God. I felt a little like a modern day Joseph. I got the draft made and took it back to the Secretary at church - mission accomplished!

That night Harold invited André and Aphelia over to the main house so he could ask them about taking over the restaurant. André felt honoured and Aphelia surprised us. We never knew what Aphelia had studied in college and had assumed it was business and office because she worked in Administration. In fact we learnt that night that she had majored in Food and Nutrition and was a qualified dietitian. Also, one of her dreams was to get into the food business. They thought that Harold's idea was divinely orchestrated. They took the news in good faith and could hardly stop thanking Harold for his kindness. They eagerly looked forward to learning the rudiments of running the business from him. Harold did promise me that he would treat my children as though they were his and he made good on that promise.

Soon after this, Anton closed on the purchase of a home, having recovered nicely from wasting his money on women. He needed some more cash for legal fees and did not even call me, but consulted Harold. They left me completely out of it and Harold did what any father would do. He is a fantastic husband and though he has no children of his own, he is definitely a father. I could see him spoiling the grandchildren already.

I am probably sounding like a broken record talking about how great my God is, but I cannot seem to stop because as soon as one miracle was finished another followed close behind. I am grounded in Christ, wrapped up, tied up, tangled up in Jesus and He was not yet finished with me – not by a long shot!

Aphelia went into labour early in July and had a beautiful baby girl. She called her Destiny, a rather lovely name, I thought. Every time they called her name they would be reminded of the road they took to this destination. Their relationship grew stronger each day and I became even more proud of my son and daughter-in-law.

When I called Sonja to say that Destiny had arrived, she also had some terrific news for me. She was returning to Trinidad, having completed the project earlier than she had expected. I was elated. We began planning her return immediately since she only had a couple months left in New York.

On hearing the news of Sonja's return, Harold came up with another fantastic idea and I could hardly believe my ears when he revealed it. Although we agreed to use his condominium as a second home, we honestly had not slept a single night there since the wedding. He was beginning to think that it did not make sense anymore. He asked me if I thought Sonja would be interested in purchasing his house. Sonja and I did talk about finding a place for her to live but made no attempts to look just yet. I had asked her the first chance I got and she agreed. I had been there only a few times but I was able to describe it to her. I do not like condominiums much but she lived in New York long enough to become quite accustomed to homes like that. She was thrilled. Harold and I cleared out the house in stages and fit Harold into my house.

Sonja had sold or donated almost everything she owned, keeping only a few personal belongings. I insisted that she stay with us until she completely turned the new place into her home. She had arrived in the middle of September causing another occasion for this family to get together again. Aphelia waited for her mother before dedicating the baby; so Destiny was dedicated early that October. She had two handsome godfathers who also were her Uncles; Aphelia's cousin, Laura and an ex-coworker, Maria, stood as godmothers. We then hosted the entire crew at home with a fine lunch which Sonja and I cooked.

Anton was not really looking himself at all the entire time we were together that day. I was sitting on the porch when he came so we could talk. I could see that something was troubling him deeply and I became concerned.

"Mom, how come you did not even ask me what's wrong?" he asked knowing full well that I did notice.

"Well, aren't you a big baby today? I was just waiting for the right time. In fact I was about to send the space ship to get you"

"Joanne and I broke up."

"Is that the reason you're so distant?" I asked knowing that it had to be more. Anton could handle break-ups; not saying that he would not be sad but I knew he could.

"That and some more," he replied with a deep sigh as he revealed the whole truth. "She was pregnant. She had an abortion. I now know how André felt that day when Aphelia revealed she had done the same thing. Why do women feel like they have the final say on these things? We were living together. We had plans for the future and I did not treat her badly, Mom. I swear I did my best."

"I am really sorry, Anton, but you have to be careful. Please, do not bring children into this world outside of marriage." He was quite disturbed and I sensed that there was even more to the cause of his sorrow.

"Are you sure that child was yours?"

"Mom, why do you always...," he started to say something but stopped. "You knew something, didn't you?

"I suspected."

"And you did not tell me because…"

"I just did not want to judge her, that's all."

"Oh, my dear mother; we just cannot fool you at all. We are so transparent. Well, I honestly cannot say for sure but she confessed to being with her ex-boyfriend."

"Son, you may never know what God has preserved you from, so just deal with the hurt and move on."

"Yeah, I know. I really did love her though."

"If you found one you will find another."

"Do you think this is payback for my behavior?"

"Choices do have consequences, but I cannot say that it's payback. Just don't be drawn back into a promiscuous lifestyle again, okay?"

"Yeah, Mom, I won't."

"By the way, honey, when are you going to give your life to Jesus? He will take that hurt and make it feel like nothing happened."

"Soon, Mother, soon."

"We do not know the day nor the hour that He will return, your soon may still be too late. What about now?"

Anton responded favourably and I prayed with him and for him. I would like to see all my children come to Christ. I saw God begin to work on Anton that same day. He still had problems with sex, but had settled into a monogamous relationship and was not promiscuous anymore. I was glad about that; I had to understand, not that I'm making excuses for him because it is still sinful. In any event, only Anton can make the choice; then God will deliver him totally. As I prayed, I felt like chains were being broken; he wept in response to the power of God that seemed so rich and real on that porch. I praised God as I remembered His promises. He did say that if we believe on Him we will be saved and our household.

Anthony was doing fine and he was quiet as usual. Still waters do run deep. He had less than a year to complete his studies and was on his way to becoming Dr. Anthony Graham. We were overjoyed at his accomplishments. He too testified that he was doing a lot more praying and felt like he trusted God to help him through although he was not completely devoted to Him. I prayed daily for total commitment.

Sonja moved into her home a month later and she settled in quite nicely. I loved the décor; it was rich - a fine place. Her house warming party was very small, just the two of us. We prayed and blessed the home ourselves and breaking the seal of Eva wine we toasted to a friendship that had spanned forty years and counting. Harold came to pick me up around ten o'clock. I asked her if she would be okay and she looked at me with disdain.

"Since when have I ever had a problem being alone, girl?"

"Jus' asking," I said as I hugged her and said goodbye.

Sonja started attending our church, eventually making it her home church as well. She also decided to join the evangelistic team that visited the hospitals and this was another thing that we did together. I saw my friend as I had never seen her before. She prayed with authority in Jesus Christ, not wavering in her faith in

God's power to heal and deliver. She was not afraid nor was she ashamed of the Gospel of Jesus Christ. As she spoke with the patients at the various institutions you could see the sincerity and genuineness in her ministry.

One Sunday the group was scheduled to visit Caura Hospital, an institution in East Trinidad where they treated patients with tuberculosis and full blown AIDS. We spent the entire afternoon praying for the patients and sharing with them the importance of giving their lives to Christ. One of the patients was guarded by a police officer and so we did not get too close to him. We were surprised as we passed by and the patient faintly called my name. I looked around wondering who it was that knew me. I did not recognise the man at all from the distance and asked the police officer to get closer to him. I was doing great until I realised who he was - Gerard Maxwell! I backed off slowly. The other ladies were curious as to who this man was. My eyes filled with tears, my heart beating to a loud drum, my mind racing back into the past. Seeing him brought back everything: the kidnapping, the abuse and consequent death of my son. It was as though it had happened yesterday. Pastor Monica held me and I whispered to her that he was the man who had kidnapped Anderson and had given him the AIDS virus.

"Here's your chance, Melinda," she said, as confident as she was that her name was Monica.

"My chance for what?" I replied, having no intentions of getting any closer to this demon.

"To forgive him in person."

Had I forgiven him or had I just forgotten about him? I wanted to finish him off - that I knew for certain. If I were not a prisoner of Christ, I would have done that for sure, but Jesus' love engulfed me and God did deliver me. If I wanted proof at all of God's power in my life, I would be telling Gerard to his face that I had forgiven him.

I walked slowly to his bed once more; Sonja on one side and Pastor Monica on the other. They both knew that I had been touched by the power of God and that I wanted to please Him more than anything else in this world. He had given my life new meaning; I sang a different song now, one of victory and of praise.

'I can do this,' I said to myself, as I felt a tear welling up in me once again. I quickly replaced it with a shout in my heart: "Hallelujah!" Then I stood right beside Gerard. I did not just say the words, 'I forgive you', I spoke with him and got him to respond. God did it! I felt it - and though I would never forget what happened, I forgave him.

'How are you doing, Gerard?" I genuinely asked as I felt my spirit release love and compassion.

"Not good, Mrs. Graham. I may not make it through the night."

"I am now Mrs. Cave. I am married to the same man that broke your door down."

A smile accompanied that statement and he returned the smile faintly not knowing whether it would hurt me or if we could now actually talk to each other, forgetting the past. He was obviously repentant and I listened to him as he spoke. The other members in the group slowly gathered around his bed as well.

"I am sorry for what I did to you and to Anderson," he began, stopping every now and again to cough.

"I knew what I was doing but I was so hurt myself and

so I did not care. I made others hurt as much as I did."

"Do you know that Andy died?"

"No. I had no idea, what happened?"

I told him what happened to Andy and he was moved to tears. He knew that he had given him the virus. He said that Keith had made him use condoms and he asked if Keith was spared. I said he was. I thought about George a little now; he was nasty up to the minute of his death but Gerard was remorseful. Although he could hardly speak, he kept saying how sorry he was.

"Gerard, I forgive you. I must forgive you in order for God to forgive me my wrongs. I forgive you."

"Thank you," he whispered, his abdomen sinking far into the ribcage as he took a deep breath. He was just skin and bones; his eyes were popping out of his head as there was no flesh to cushion them. As he lay there dying, we led him to Christ and then he let us in on the secret that had motivated him to be so evilly inclined.

It turned out that when Gerard was just nine years old his mother left him to find a better life in America. She had placed him in the hands of his dead father's brother who promised to keep him until she came back home. His uncle was a monster, a drug addict who sold Gerard to the pushers and whosoever will, for drugs. He was too young to defend himself and while his mother was told that he was doing great, he was actually being raped daily by many different people. Gerard's mom returned and took him from the uncle ten months later but it was already too late, the damage was done. At first, she was clueless as to what had happened to her son, but those events scarred him for life. He contracted the disease and grew up a bitter and angry man who did the same to others. He in turn abused young boys. He told us that he was not homosexual at all; he targeted young boys for revenge. His victims lived because he wanted them to feel the pain he felt and only killed the twin boys because they had attacked him and he defended himself. He was now in an advanced stage of pneumonia and they had to transfer him to Caura from Golden Grove Prison where he was serving a life sentence.

"I was sentenced to life in prison when they caught me and that I deserved but I was sentenced to death when I was yet an innocent little child and that I could not accept."

Those words tore my heart into pieces. I felt for this man and I knew that Jesus died for him, too. I told him that he must believe that God had forgiven him and that he could be in heaven with Jesus.

We watched Gerard die that evening and knowing that God wishes that none perish I was glad that we were able to reach him even if it was on his death bed. As we turned to leave, Pastor Monica asked me how I was doing and I answered her candidly when I said, "I am relieved."

The event had me thinking a lot about my purpose. Why did God preserve me? I too was exposed to a multiplicity of sex partners by George's indiscretion, yet I did not get any sexually transmitted diseases. I was enjoying my life; I knew that God had His hand upon me. However, as I thought more and more as to why God created us, why he created me, to be more specific, I began to feel like there was still a lot more to live for.

Pastor Monica told her husband about the experience we had had at the hospital. He then called me to ask if I would share my testimony at church the next Sunday and I agreed. It was going to be the first time that I would speak publicly about my life and the first time that the boys would hear my plight. I gave it over to God in prayer asking Him to guide me and to speak through me. My life experiences had to be for a purpose; if so, then people must hear of the experience in order for the purpose to be materialized.

I felt God's strength and power as I stood in front of the congregation. My eyes wandered for a few quick seconds; the church looked different from that vantage point. Every eye was fixed on me in great anticipation of what I was about to share. I could almost see their spirits waiting to hear something that would help them to go through the coming week. 'This is so much pressure,' I thought to myself; the responsibility is fierce and one sentence can make or break someone's expectations of what 'church' really is. If the minister has not done it before, here is when he asks God to use his eyes, hands, speech and heart, to expound words of wisdom and encouragement to the ears and the hearts of the people in the congregation.

I wondered how André would respond. He knew that I had been abused; he had revealed it to me a couple years ago. However, we had never discussed details. I was ready and believed that I was empowered by the Holy Spirit not just to talk but to minister. I felt like the Samaritan woman at the well when Jesus touched her. She could not care less what anybody else thought; she had a story to tell and was brazen in her approach.

For about twenty minutes or so I spoke openly, withholding sensitive details, of course, about the trauma I suffered under George's hands and how Andy's death overwhelmed me; but more importantly, I spoke about how God had delivered me. I emphasized the power of forgiveness and how my unwillingness to forgive at first produced devastating effects on my life in general but as I released those who had hurt me, I felt like weights drop with every step that I took in life. It was only then I was able to break out of the inevitable prison. One must yield to God and live – truly live.

I was amazed to see how God was using my testimony to draw men to Him. As I spoke, the ushers distributed napkins to people who were crying and weeping. As I ministered under the anointing, people reached out to God for His power and the peace that it brings. They were applying it to their situations, releasing themselves, from their own prison. I wrapped it up. I knew I had said enough and I felt led by God to address the congregation directly at this point. I softly began to sing Martha Minuzzi's, 'There is a sweet anointing in the sanctuary'. The musicians accompanied me, maintaining the softness in the atmosphere, and I beckoned to the worship leader to take over the song. I walked over to where Pastor sat and told him what I wanted to do. He consented and stood with me and so did Pastor Monica. He made the call and the altar was filled in less than a minute.

The rest of the service was used to pray for people as they liberated themselves through worship to God. His presence was strong and commandingly awesome. He was delivering His people; unlocking chains of bondage and replacing them with His loving arms. I could stand no more on my feet. As I worshipped I felt the power of God overwhelm me. I got on my knees bowing in worship, tears of joy flowing from my eyes, my hands lifted in surrender to the Blessed Holy Spirit. Sweet communion with God is indescribably awesome. When Jesus touches you He changes you. Holy is the Lord, indeed.

Pastor Joseph allowed the members to remain basking in the presence of God while the worship team continued to sing softly. After a few minutes they began walking back to their seats. André did not move with the crowd; he remained at the altar embracing a young man, speaking in an unknown tongue as tears streamed down his face. Harold stood behind them supporting this majestic move of God. André was facing the altar and at first I did not know who the man was but soon recognised my son, Anton. He had given his life to Christ a few weeks ago at home. He was present at church that day. He did not call to say that he was coming. Maybe that was a good thing as I might have tried to stop him so he wouldn't hear my real story. However, God used our own story to deliver Anton that day. I thanked God, making certain to mention that Anthony was still not completely there yet. I joined the two and hugged them, as the congregation continued to pray and praise.

God took over the service that day. Pastor's agenda was thrown out the window and the Holy Spirit had preeminence. God truly was in control! I could have stayed there forever.

Epilogue

Ten years later

From Evans to Graham to Cave: the genes of three different men have contributed to the existence of the occupants of this home. I was born here as Melinda Caren Evans. I grew up here, and both my husbands joined me in this home. My children know this house and now their children have embraced the love that emanates from this home, a place we have fashioned to foster family values. I often wondered what it would have been like to live somewhere else, but this is my home. Everything that was pleasing to me, along with all the tumultuous and heart-piercing sorrows have happened right here. God does turn your mourning into dancing again!

Ten years ago I broke out of the dreadful prison I was in: one characterized by abuse, hostility and evil; a life that my dead, ex-husband had inflicted on me. I found new life in Christ Jesus, my Lord, my Saviour, and my Friend. Through Him I learned to forgive everyone for the wrongs that they had committed against me, whether or not they wanted my forgiveness. Whether or not they were alive to hear me say, 'I forgive you', there is no denying that there was a peace that the act brought through its application. I learned to forgive myself and to accept the forgiveness God offered me.

I have a new husband, a man after God's own heart. Harold has shown me what 'husband' really means. The love and attention he showers on me is deeply satisfying. The support and encouragement that run alongside his adoration is the secret ingredient to our personal love story. Harold kept his promise to love me and to cherish me and now that I'm sixty years old, I believe that 'till death do us part' is something we can look forward to.

As we all go through life, we inevitably become a prisoner to something or someone. Whether it is by choice or by consequence, every man is a prisoner. If this is true and I dare you to tell me differently, we should consciously choose our 'prison'. (Hold on: you'll soon understand what I mean.) We should not permit a prison to choose us. If we fail to stand for something, we will obviously fall for anything.

My life has new meaning now and as I continue to live with purpose, I know that I have chosen my 'prison' and have become a true prisoner of Christ. But guess what? I love every minute of it. In Christ I have freedom; not freedom to do what I want but to do what He wants – to do what is right. Prisoners in the natural are given daily instructions. They never decide on their own menus, they are told when to eat, what to eat and even how to eat it. They do not choose their daily jobs; even the once well-respected lawyers and doctors who are imprisoned become labourers one day, then janitors the next. All truths are parallel; being a prisoner of Christ simply means that I depend on Christ for daily instructions. What job do You want me to do today, Lord? Where should I go? Your Word is my food, so what shall I eat today? Shall I ingest poetry or praise, history or hermeneutics? One might be tempted to ask, 'Is that freedom?" Yes, it is; I do declare. When we come into the full understanding of the why, when, where, and who, we will know what freedom is. Freedom is life in Jesus Christ.

It was a sad day when we lost Anderson to suicide. Can a mother ever forget the trauma that goes along with that? When a piece of your heart is ripped from its cavity but you have the will to live, you do; but who can truly mend the heart but Jesus? It is difficult to think that Anderson is probably experiencing torment. I really did not know what he did with Jesus at all. He came to church often but I never saw him publicly give his life to Christ. Knowing that he took his own life is also difficult to think about. Suicide is a permanent solution to a temporary problem. One cannot reverse the decision for it is the murder of oneself and the scripture states: Thou shall not kill. Who knows if there was time for repentance?

André and Aphelia added Darius to their family. Destiny was very happy to have a little brother. My dear son and his wife have stepped into Harold's shoes, taking complete ownership of the restaurant. Harold and I go there for dinner now and again and we are pleased with the job they are doing. Destiny and Darius both inherited the family talent of singing. You should hear these little ones sing to God; at ten and eight they are already shaping up to be a brother and sister duo like Bebe and Cece Winans.

My other two sons have since married as well and have kids of their own so I now have five grandchildren. Anton married Cindy, a beautiful young woman from our church and they have one child, Micah. I can say Anton is truly delivered. He battled that sexual addiction until Jesus delivered him, totally and completely. It did not matter how many times he tried on his own, satan's hold was strong. If Anton had not yielded to Jesus he would never have been freed from his prison. I still don't know how he escaped HIV infection or any other sexually transmitted diseases. Only God preserved him!

Dr. Anthony Graham finally unlocked his chains as well. He met Kimberley at Harold's Restaurant and the two became inseparable. They dated for two years before getting married. They now have two children, Joel and Joshua. He got his voice back and the child, who had hid himself away when his father rejected him, unlocked the prison doors and broke free.

Each member of my family now knows Christ as Lord and Saviour. No one escaped as Harold and I made certain to declare daily: 'As for me and my house, we will serve the Lord.'

Sonja, my best friend since we were kids, has stood by my side through it all. She never married though. She really would have liked to, but made up her mind that she wouldn't fall for the 'Before none, any' syndrome. Though the prospects were many, she decided to remain unmarried, pleasing God each step of the way.

I share my testimony with various groups and institutions across this beautiful twin island Republic and have been to two other Caribbean islands for the purpose of ministry. I am convinced that God allows us to go through life, gathering experiences and having victories so we can one day be an example to someone who is suffering a similar fate. I have learned to appreciate how God used the trials in my life to make a difference in the lives of others. I refer to those trials as my classroom and I am reminded daily that this life is not my own.

God created us to serve Him, but he did not want a squad of robotic creatures. He wanted a people who would use the privilege of choice. I have chosen Him. I have decided to follow Jesus - to be His servant, His prisoner.

Today and for always, I am, happily, a prisoner of the Lord Jesus Christ.

Inspirational Reading

Though this book is fiction, it brings to life a powerful truth. The main character, Melinda, mentioned a book "Forgiveness Unlimited". This is a real book written by Apostle Emanuel Vivian Duncan. Add this book to your library. Forgiveness truly unlocks prison doors. Available at Exousia Book & Gift Centre, Trinidad. (1 868 695 7892)

The writer of the foreword of Prisoners is a remarkable woman. A woman of integrity and substance. Apostle Jemma Duncan is also a prolific writer like her husband Apostle Vivian. In this book, I am Woman, Apostle Jemma tells all how to be "Woman". Here she also bravely tells her story which I know will liberate you. Available at Exousia Book & Gift Centre, Trinidad. (1 868 695 7892)

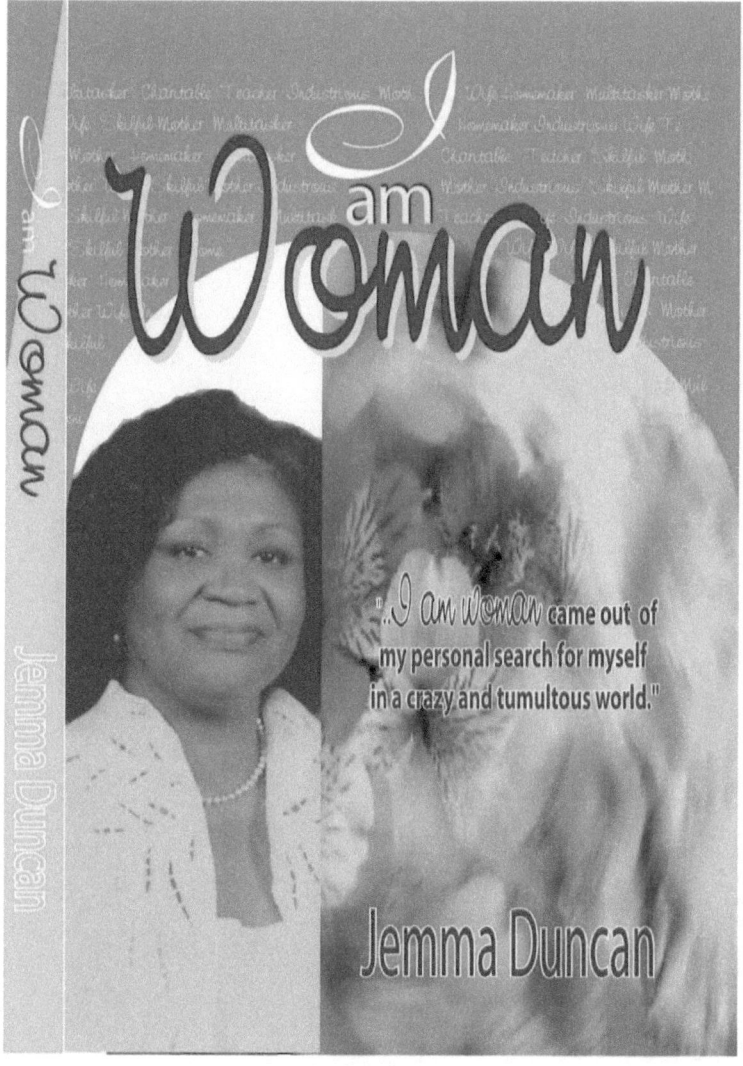

www.ingramcontent.com/pod-product-compliance
Lightning Source LLC
Chambersburg PA
CBHW020315200626
46814CB00006BA/2258